DANIEL KIPPS

Tales of Cthulhu and Other Gods of Old

Volume 1

"The most merciful thing in the world,
I think, is the inability of the human
mind to correlate all its contents. We
live on a placid island of ignorance in
the midst of black seas of the infinity,
and it was not meant that we should
voyage far."

H. P. Lovecraft, The Call of
Cthulhu and Other Weird
Stories

Contents

Foreword

Hello there, brave reader.

First off… **thank you.** If you're holding this book, you're either a fan of cosmic horror like me, or the promise of monsters, madness, and maybe a little too much curiosity for your own good, have lured you in. Either way, welcome.

I've always been fascinated by the kind of horror that *lingers*. Not the jump scares or gore (though those have their place), but the kind that worms its way into your mind and festers. The kind that whispers, *what if the world is far older, darker, and more unknowable than we ever imagined?* That's where **Lovecraftian horror** comes in… and let me tell you, I've been hooked for years.

The stories in this collection are my own tribute to that brand of unease. They're inspired by the **Cthulhu Mythos** and the pantheon of **Old Gods**, but I'll say right now, don't expect a roll call of Great Old Ones in every tale. These stories aren't so much about the gods themselves as they are about their shadow. About what it feels like when something vast and ancient passes just beyond the corner of your vision, and you're left wondering whether you even saw anything at all - the ancient beings that were around before humans, before our world and even before space and time.

That said, if you're looking for a story that leans full-tilt into the mythos, you'll definitely want to check out *'The Sleeper's*

Breath'. That one dives, literally, deep into the dark heart of a very familiar god. You'll know which one.

Elsewhere in the collection, things are a little more ambiguous. Take the story of *'Stranger at the Station'*, where you could argue (and I certainly would) that the figure haunting that story is a manifestation of Nyarlathotep, *The Black Man,* in one of his more disturbing forms who is subtly out to cause cruelty and madness. But again, it's all suggestion, implication, atmosphere. That's what I love most about this kind of horror. It's not always about spelling things out, it's about making you feel something ancient is watching. Listening. Waiting.

Genre-wise, you're going to find a mix in here. Some of the stories are straight-up **sci-fi horror**, such as *'The Final Log'*, with cold metal corridors and things that shouldn't breathe in the vacuum of space. Others fall into **dark fantasy**, such as the story *'Whispers Beneath the Mountain'*, where the world feels a little off, a little too cruel, and where an imprisoned god is wreaking havoc on the nearby village and it's up to a band of adventurers, fueled by a cleric's vision, to free him. There's even the occasional psychological horror told from the first-person perspective of an eight-year-old boy, Jack, in *'The Invitation'*, whereby you get to see the unraveling of a manipulation of ritual sacrifice from Jack's own eyes.

One special mention has to be the story about the Knights Templar, *'Ancient One Below'*. It was actually a finalist in an international writing competition. The story itself came to me on a recent trip to Transylvania, whereby I discovered in Bran Castle that there used to be an ancient, wooden fortress which burned down in mysterious circumstances… So it's fair to say that the story uses real world, historical facts to give credibility to the horror within. Of course, my mind jumped to grim reasons as to why the fire engulfed the fortress, and I hope you enjoy what my brain came up with… spoilers - it might be something to do with an old god.

The creation of these short stories has been immensely enjoyable and I owe a lot to my loving partner, who has supported me through this journey. I couldn't have done it without you. Thank you. You know who you are.

I wrote these stories because I love this stuff. I love the creeping dread, the whispers from the void. The idea that behind the stars lie gods too vast and alien for us to comprehend. If any of that excites or terrifies you, then you're exactly where you need to be. If, when you've finished reading, you enjoyed the collection, **a review would be amazing** (anywhere online or even just word-of-mouth!). They really do help and I have a lot more stories to tell…

Enjoy the descent and keep an eye out for volume two.

Daniel

The Dark Road Near Innsmouth

om's hands trembled on the steering wheel as the car jolted violently, a sickening thud echoing through the night. "What the hell was that?" Holly snapped, her voice sharp with accusation, but all Tom could do was stare into the darkness ahead, the twisted shapes of the ancient forest closing in around them. Something lay motionless in the road behind the car; he knew it, just beyond the reach of the taillights, and his heart pounded with sheer dread. Too afraid to look in the rear-view mirror. Too scared to turn around. Too petrified to even blink. What had he done?

Was Holly's constant arguing in his right ear so bad that he lost concentration? Was his mind still on that awful party? Did it matter? Did it actually matter at all?

For a split second, everything felt so silent. Tom felt guilty for this next thought, but he thought it, nonetheless. It felt… *nice*. It felt *peaceful*. Maybe he could drive away and pretend nothing happened. I mean, who would know? They were driving in the ass end of nowhere. Some shortcut this turned out to be. Then normality returned with *that* voice he had put up with for the last twenty miles.

"What the heck have you done, Tom?!" Holly yelled. Her

shrill voice cutting through the silence. "Did you actually hit something back there?"

"Erm. Yes, I think. *Maybe*." Tom fumbled the words out.

"You think? Were you even looking at the road?"

Tom had been. He reckons he was probably staring through the road, trying to block out the shouting and screaming he hated. All they seemed to do lately was argue, and Tom would have done anything to fix that, but he couldn't ever bring himself to fight back. When he refused to engage in the argument, it wound Holly up more, and she'd often accuse him of being a spineless coward. He wasn't a coward, damn it!

"*I* can't believe *I've* been involved in an accident!" Holly continued.

Holly always made it about her; she was very good at flipping things around like that. Tom gripped the wheel tighter, his knuckles turning white. Was it from rage? Was he feeling rage towards his soon-to-be fiancée? Tonight was going to be the night as well. He would finally pop the question, mainly because he thought she'd treat him better if he proposed, but what happened at the party completely ruined any chances.

For a moment, Tom welcomed the rage; it replaced the panic and fear of the accident. His death grip released. He closed his eyes, took a deep breath and said, "Maybe it was a deer..."

"It wasn't a fucking deer, Tom," Holly cut him off, her voice filled with dread. "Deer don't make that kind of sound."

For a moment, they both recalled the noise... the sickening thud, the howl of pain, the squelches. Oh god, the squelches - almost like someone slapping a wet piece of meat on a kitchen counter. Then there was a guttural croak as it finally came to a stop. Whatever it was, it could surely be in no fit state to ID them. Could he drive away? Leave all this mess behind?

The realization of what those noises meant hit them both at the same time, and Tom felt the blood drain from his face. Then he remembered the party and how he couldn't stand up for Holly like a decent human would have. He remembered being called a coward by her and how much it always hurt when she did that. He'll show her…

Tom unbuckled his seat belt with trembling fingers and reached for the door handle. "I need to check," he said, though his voice was barely more than a whisper.

"Are you insane? You're just going to get out there and…"

"Holly, I have to see what it is. What if it's a person?" His mind was a whirlwind of terror and guilt, the weight of his cowardice pressing down on him like never before. But he couldn't ignore this. He had to know what he had hit and, more importantly, he had to show her he was a *real* man.

Holly rolled her eyes. "So now you want to be brave? Where was *this* Tom at the party, hmm? Where was my knight in shining armor when that guy said I was heartless?"

"He was drunk. I wouldn't pick a fight with a drunk guy, Holly. Anyway, stop talking about that god damned party; we're in trouble here."

"Ugh, I can't believe you Tom! If word ever gets out that I was involved in an accident where someone got hurt, what do you think would happen to Sweetie Paws?!"

That god damn 'Sweetie Paws' again. It was Holly's attempt at working from home - creating cakes for pets. She probably sold two doggie cupcakes in the last few months, so it wasn't lucrative by any stretch of the imagination, but it kept her busy. It kept her focused on something other than his flaws, which is why he indulged her, for the most part. The cakes were actually good! Well, when she made human ones, anyway. She definitely had a skill there. Lately, however, everything has become about 'the brand,' probably because she was watching some jumped-up teen influencer on social media. It just meant that whenever he heard the words 'Sweetie Paws', his skin would crawl. And what a place to bring up her cake business?! How could she be thinking about that now?

Tom clenched his teeth. He'd rather be out of the car with whatever lay twenty feet behind him than be in here another second. He may end up saying something that would cause further escalation.

No, it's *always safer to walk away* in times like this...

"I'm just going to check; maybe I can help?" Tom stepped outside and shut the door. There was that sound again, or lack of sound. Pure forest road silence. Bliss! It would have been an enjoyable place to gaze up at the stars if it wasn't for the fact that there was a body somewhere back there, in the darkness. What surprised him most was the wafting, pungent, fishy smell. It must have been from the town of Innsmouth, a few miles away. Tom's never been, nor knows anyone who had, but with the main road out, this forest detour that brought them close to that fishing town was the only other way to return home to Ipswich. There were some strange rumors about that place...

Tom grabbed his phone, thumbed on the light, and turned towards the back of the car. With his other hand, he felt the engagement ring box in his left pocket. He *was* brave; he could do this. She'll see...

The body lay only twenty feet behind the car, but it seemed so much further to Tom. The red tail lights made everything seem even more surreal, as if everything was just some crazy dream he was bound to wake up from soon. No. This *was* happening. The proof was there, at the very edge of where the red light stopped. All Tom could see were two feet poking out of the darkness. Feet! Oh god, it *was* a human.

Tom edged closer. The light from the phone slowly moved up the body with every step, revealing filthy workman-style trousers, smeared with grease and juices from God knows what, containing two thick, tree trunk-like thighs. No wonder the sound of the hit was so loud. This guy was a beast. Not overly tall, but squat and stocky. Tom took another hesitant step forward, his heart pounding in his chest. He lifted the torchlight higher and saw the figure wearing a rough-knitted jumper. Blood pooled around the body, glistening in the bright light of the phone's torch. Tom was mere feet away now, and the light could finally reveal the full extent of the carnage - a mangled, twisted human body. Well... human-*ish*. Something seemed off about the shape - various bumps and ridges along the back were visible through the blood-stained jumper, which Tom initially put down to broken bones or dislodged vertebrae.

"Geez..." The words escaped his lips in a strangled gasp as he covered his nose. That smell was so strong, being this close to the body, like a ten-day-old fish left in the sun. It came from this poor soul, laying on the road and invaded his nostrils the closer he got. Maybe he used to work down on the docks?

"Tom?" Holly's voice called out from the car, but it sounded distant, as if coming from another world. "What is it? What do you see?"

"It's OK, Holly. *I'm* dealing with it."

Tom swallowed hard, bile rising in his throat as he forced himself to crouch down to inspect the disfigured body. The figure was a man, his worn clothes ragged and soaked with blood. Maybe it was just a hobo? That might explain the smell. Perhaps no one would even miss him? While inspecting the disfigured body, Tom observed that the man's face was obscured and twisted at an unnatural angle. With a sick certainty, he knew that there was no saving him.

Tom stood up. There was no point examining any further; this guy was dead, so he backed away, his breaths coming in short, panicked gasps. "He's… he's dead, Holly."

A heavy silence followed his words. Tom turned and staggered back to the car, his legs weak and unsteady, but with every step, the situation seemed less dire than he first thought. Sure, it was a terrible accident, but it was only a hobo. So what? People have accidents all the time. They could be out of here in two minutes, and no one would ever know. But before he could reach the door, Holly was out of the car, rushing towards him.

"Wait, Holly, don't—"

But she was already past him, her phone in hand, the light trembling as she ran towards the body.

"Holly, no!" Tom grabbed her arm, pulling her back. "There's no point… I mean, we have to go…"

Holly turned, glaring at him with a mixture of anger and disbelief. "What are you talking about? We can't just leave him here! What's wrong with you, Tom?"

Tom couldn't believe it. Holly was thinking of someone else for a change. Sure, it was some stinky, dead hobo and not his long-suffering partner of twelve years, but it surprised Tom regardless. To this day, Tom still regrets the words that next came out of his mouth. He could have said something else if he knew what would happen in the next few minutes.

"…but what about Sweetie Paws, Holly?"

"How dare you!" she snapped back.

She was correct; what was he thinking? Tom felt a wave of

panic washing over him. His mind raced, thoughts tumbling over one another in a chaotic mess.

"But… what if they think it was *our* fault? What if we go to jail? Holly, we can't stay here we need…"

Before he could finish, Holly jerked her arm free and stepped towards the body. "Tom, stop being such a co…"

A sudden, wet, gurgling noise that rose from the figure on the ground cut her words short. Both of them froze, their eyes wide with horror as the man's body twitched, his limbs jerking in unnatural spasms. Tom's breath caught in his throat, and his mind screamed to run, but he found himself rooted to the spot. He watched in paralyzed terror as the man's twisted neck snapped back into place with a sickening crack, and his head slowly turned to face them.

"Holy shit," Holly couldn't move and stood, transfixed, on the creature.

The eyes that stared up at her were not human. They were large, bulbous, and glistening, like the eyes of some deep-sea creature. Wet, pale, green skin shone against the red tail lights as the thing sat up, and Tom saw gills under a rip in its jumper. The thing had gills?! This was no human… but it wasn't entirely monstrous, either. It was a hybrid thing - as if someone took a fisherman and mixed it with a sea beast from the ocean floor. Then, in a split second, the creature's mouth flew open far wider than any human's should, revealing rows of sharp, needle-like teeth. And with a low, guttural growl, he emitted a deep sound from his throat. A sound that sent a chill down Tom's spine.

"Iä! Iä! Cthulhu fhtagn!"

Oh Christ, that noise it made. The world around Tom spun, everything blurring into one dark smear as he stumbled backward, but somehow, he didn't pass out. The thing somehow sounded more hideous than it looked. His mind couldn't understand what his senses were telling him. The image of that creature was horrific, but the noise still haunts Tom's dreams to this day. It was closer to a frog's croak than anything uttered by a human tongue. Before he knew it, Tom had taken five steps back towards the car while Holly stood a few inches from the monster.

"Holly, *get back,*" Tom weakly uttered, trying to break her free of the paralysis verbally. "...*Please?*"

But it was too late...

The creature lunged at Holly with speed and ferocity, that defied its earlier stillness. A clawed, webbed hand wrapped around her leg, letting out a bone-chilling squeal. Holly screamed, thrashing wildly as she tried to free herself, but the creature's grip was too firm, and as the two-inch-long claws sunk into her thigh, she let out a high-pitched howl of pain. The claws ripped down her leg, causing Holly to buckle and tumble onto the asphalt.

Tom's heart pounded in his chest as he watched in horror, unable to move or think. He saw the monster climb on top of Holly, a huge smile plastered across that giant angler fish-like mouth. The creature brought down his claws over and over again, tearing into Holly's flesh and spewing her blood across the asphalt. Her screams were deafening, filled with pain and primal terror, but Tom couldn't bring himself to do anything but watch.

"Tom! Help me!" Holly's voice was desperate, pleading, her mouth filled with blood, as she reached out towards him. "Please, T-T-Tom!"

Tom did nothing. How could he? He just stood there, frozen to the spot. Is this what it's come to, that he must watch his loved one be ripped to shreds as punishment for years of cowardice? Then a thought came to him: even if he could get his legs working again, what good would it do? Surely, the thing would turn on him, and the creature would get two meals out of this accident. Holly wouldn't want that, would she? No, she'd like him to be safe, to get away, and to report this horrific incident. Then he could send help, and everything would be OK.

No, it's *always safer to walk away* in times like this…

The creature rose back up to his feet and hooked his slimy, webbed hand into the roof of Holly's mouth, its claws slicing through flesh and bone. Holly wriggled and writhed, like a fish caught on a hook, as the monster turned to stare at Tom as if to check if he was going to do anything, but of course, he wasn't; he had already made his mind up.

The thing opened his bloody mouth and said, "Iä! Iä! Cthulhu fhtagn! Ph'nglui mglw'nafh Cthulhu R'lyeh wgah'nagl fhtagn!".

"Argh," Tom grabbed his head in his hands. Those words seemed so familiar, if you can call them 'words.' They bore deep into his mind, showing him sights behind his comprehension - places so strange and grotesque yet hauntingly beautiful. Images of non-Euclidean geometry hurt his mind, causing his head to pound whenever he tried to fathom their alien construction. The sights he saw for those few seconds would forever haunt his dreams.

With the clawed fingers embedded in her mouth, Holly whimpered, "I 'oun wanna 'ie!!" tears streaming down her face and mixing with her blood and the thing's mucus.

The creature turned and started to drag Holly out of the red light, her legs thrashing around in vain and into the darkness until the dark entirely engulfed her. Out of sight, but never out of mind.

Tom was standing alone - just him, the car, and a myriad of blood, piss, and mucus which had sprayed and pooled around the road. In the distance, Holly's screams were getting quieter and more distant as the thing dragged its trophy back towards Innsmouth. Soon, the horrific sound was gone and all that remained was that still, peaceful silence.

Suddenly, power returned to his legs. He turned, ran back to the car, fumbled for the door handle, threw it open, and jumped in. He could still smell her in here. The fishy smell was no longer present; "Oh god, Holly! My poor Holly!". His breath came in short, ragged gasps as he stared wide-eyed at the road ahead. Just what the hell was that thing? How could he leave Holly back there? Why didn't he help her? The answer was obvious. He fired up the engine and floored it.

With tears streaming down his face, he finally accepted what he was - a coward. Holly had been right all along.

They *all* had.

The Invitation

I'm going to open these stupid letters…

Evelyn always gets it wrong.

She's the worst mail woman ever.

Three times she has given us mail meant for the house across the road.

We're fifty-three Hill Drive, not fifty-two!

I keep telling her, but she doesn't listen.

No one listens to me.

They keep saying I'm just a kid, but I'm almost nine. I'm not a kid.

Enough is enough.

I'm responsible and will sort this mess out myself.

Just like a hero.

I closed my bedroom door, grabbed the three letters from under my bed, and remembered how they all came to me over the last week…

Day One - The First Letter

Ding Dong.

The door!

Yes! It could be the post!

My comic might finally arrive today - Detective Gary, the world's best boy detective!

It's issue 150, and I've been waiting *ages* to see what happens to Gary and the evil Dr. Sludge.

Last time we saw Gary, Dr. Sludge and his baddies had wrapped his hands with duct tape and held him prisoner.

How could he escape that?!

Ding Dong. BANG, BANG, BANG.

The bangs knock me out of my daydream.

I got so excited that I realized I had just been standing on the landing in my own little world.

Mom says I do that a lot.

Hey, why isn't anyone answering the door?

Mom must be sleeping on the couch again with one of her nasty headaches.

"I'll get it!" I whispered and ran down the stairs, three at a time.

I can see the Mail man's uniform through the frosted glass in our front door.

It IS the post!

I fling the door open. "Hi Harry…. oh".

It's not Harry.

But it has *always* been Harry.

"Hello Dearie, I think I have some post for you."

She looked old.

Much older than Harry.

She had a big smile and bent down to me as she handed me the mail.

Why didn't she post them through the letterbox?

"...You're not Harry."

She chuckled, correcting me. "Haha, no. I'm not Harry. I'm Evelyn, the new mail woman in town. First day on the job!"

I stared at her.

Confused.

Where's Harry?

"Oh, OK... Nice to meet you. I'm Jack."

My Mom taught me that good manners are important.

"Hello there, Jack. Wow, you look like such a big, healthy boy. I reckon you must be... hm... At least twelve years old!"

That warm smile seemed to stretch even further now.

"Haha, no. I'm eight!" This made me giggle. I enjoyed being called older.

I often thought that it sucked being a kid.

"Well, bless my soul! I'd have never guessed."

She stood back up.

She stared at me for a few seconds.

Like she was examining me the way my doctor does.

It felt... *weird.*

I didn't know what to say.

"Such a good boy. Anyway, I better be getting along now. There are a lot of houses on my route. Do me a favor; make sure you enjoy those letters."

'Enjoy' them?

What did she mean?

I don't know what Mom does with the letters, but I really don't think she *enjoys* them.

Usually, she throws them away, mutters at least five different naughty words, and then gets herself a 'big drink.'

I shut the door, walked towards the kitchen, and thumbed through the letters.

No comic.

Drat.

Mom was sleeping, so I just put the letters on the kitchen table.

Then, a fancy letter slid out of the pile.

It was in a pretty, yellowish envelope with fancy, handwritten writing on the front.

Who would write to us?

Wait a minute, it was for fifty-two Hill Drive.

We're *fifty-three*!

Evelyn must have delivered to the wrong house.

Silly Evelyn.

Being a mail person was probably tricky, though. Especially on their first day.

I scooped up the fancy letter, quickly dashed back to the front door, opened it, and looked down the street.

She was nowhere to be seen.

I guess she drove away.

There are only a few other families on our street, so there is no need to hang around, I guess.

Mom says that everyone is selling up to move to the big city.

Maybe I could hold on to this letter until Evelyn returns tomorrow morning?

Hmm, it might confuse Mom though...

I know! I'll take it to my room, so my mom doesn't see it.

Then she won't get cross and rip the thing up.

She gets angry when people don't do their job properly.

She says people should be lucky to have a decent job and that she could do it better.

Anyway, it's not like I can just pop over the road and deliver it myself.

I closed the door and walked up the stairs.

Gah, it really sucked that my comic didn't come.

I slowly trudged into my room to sulk.

What was I going to do to pass the time?

This had been the worst summer ever.

Sometimes I wish I could be like Detective Gary - solving local mysteries and being a hero.

I flopped down on my bed and stared out the window.

House number fifty-two looked like a strange place.

It kinda looked like ours, but somehow older and creepier.

There were twelve steps leading up from the pavement to the big, old, wooden front door.

The outside was probably a pretty shade of green in the past, but the paint had cracked and was peeling off.

Spooky house.

I wonder if it's haunted.

It spooks me every time I walk past it on the way to school, but I've never seen the people who lived there.

I guess they only go in and out at night.

But I knew people lived there because I'd hear the cars come and go on the crunchy gravel drive, down the side of the house, while I was trying to sleep.

Someone always kept the curtains drawn, too.

Maybe their mom doesn't like the sunlight either?

I'll return the letter to Evelyn tomorrow.

I'm sure they won't mind it being a day late.

I have nothing to do but wait for tomorrow, I guess.

Day Two - Comic Day

I woke to the sound of my alarm buzzing.

A new day of nothingness in the most *boring* summer holiday of all time.

I let out a long yawn, rubbed my eyes, and then remembered that it could be a comic day!

With a gasp, I got up, threw on some clothes, brushed my teeth, and ran down the stairs.

"Morning, Jackie." my mom ruffled my hair and cuddled me as I entered the kitchen.

"Has the post been?" I instantly responded.

Feeling hopeful.

"Do you mean 'Morning, Mother'? 'It's nice to see you, Mother'?" she said with a cheeky smile.

I liked it when Mom was in a playful mood.

"Hehe, sorry, Mom. I'm just excited because Detective Gary might turn up today!"

"No post yet, poppet." As she pushed a slice of toast in my mouth.

"I *need* to pop into town this morning. Will you be OK staying here for a few hours? I know you're just a kid, but I have no choice." Mom said.

"Sure, Mom." Taking the toast out of my mouth. "And, hey, I'm *not* a kid anymore."

I hated it when people just said I was a kid.

"That's my special boy. Maybe I'll bring you back some candy to go with your comic?"

"Wahoo!"

Candy and comic?

It was the *best* day ever!

Mom crouched down in front of me. "Listen, Jack, I know things are hard right now. I'm trying my hardest. I know things will get better soon, though."

She had teary puppy dog eyes. The kind she gets when she's sad but trying to hide it.

"I just need to work a few more weeks and then we can go do something fun. Maybe Disney?"

"For real?" I almost exploded.

I had always wanted to go to Disney World.

"For real, Jack. Just give me a few weeks."

"OK Mom, you're the best!"

After breakfast, Mom grabbed her car keys, said goodbye, and left for town.

I stayed downstairs, near the front door, so I could hear when the post landed on the doormat.

I didn't want to waste a single second not reading issue 150.

Maybe I could do my chores now and get them out of the way.

The smell was awful as I walked into the lounge and picked up Mom's mess.

I counted three bottles, a pizza box, and four boxes of cigarettes.

On bad days, she would forget to tidy up, but I didn't mind helping as long as I didn't throw out the wrong thing.

I don't enjoy getting in trouble.

Ding Dong

POST!

Sprinting towards the door, I slid on the wood floor and flung it open.

"Why, if it isn't my special friend, Jack? Hello again."

It was Evelyn with that giant, warm smile again.

"Hi, Evelyn!"

Her uniform was so new.

So clean.

I could smell a strong but pleasant lavender smell coming from her.

Old people smell.

Then I remembered…

"Oh, wait there. I have something for you."

I ran to my room, grabbed the yellowish envelope, and leaped down the stairs.

I held out the envelope for her to take.

"You accidentally gave this to me yesterday, but it's for the house across the road."

"Oh, I did? What a silly thing to do. I must have read the number wrong. To be honest, I think I was slightly nervous - the first day jitters. I haven't worked a proper job in years, you see, and it's tough getting back out there. Back on the saddle, so to speak."

What saddle? Maybe she rides a bike?

She hasn't taken the envelope yet.

"That's OK. It must be a tricky job, but you'll get the hang of it."

Why hasn't she taken it?

Evelyn squatted down to my level.

"Can I ask you a huge favor? Can I trust you with something? *Something secret.*"

"Yes. Of course, I'm good at keeping secrets."

"The thing is, I made a bit of a booboo giving you that envelope, but if I take it back, I could get into a lot of trouble, and I don't want to lose my job. Could you hold on to it for me, please? Just until I've got my first week out of the way?"

This felt… *wrong*.

"But won't fifty-two be sad they didn't get their letter?"

"Oh, people lose mail all the time. They'll get it eventually, and I'm sure you'll do a great job looking after it, won't you? Please help me out?"

I am good at looking after things…

I puffed out my chest. "OK, Evelyn. You can count on me!"

"Such a good boy. Your Mom must be so proud…" she said, with an unsettling smile.

Her smile reminded me of my Gran, but it felt different, almost eerie.

"So, I noticed your mom is out, as the car isn't there. I hope you don't mind me talking to you like this? I do really enjoy our little chats. They help set me up for the day ahead. You know, I think you're a truly *extraordinary* boy."

She stood up and took a bundle of bills, ads, and magazines from her grubby postbag.

The mailbag.

I didn't notice the mailbag yesterday.

It looked so *out-of-place* now that I was examining it.

Her uniform was so fresh, but the mailbag was dirty, worn, and well-used.

It looked just like the one Harry used.

In fact, I think it probably WAS the one Harry used.

I guess they only give new people fresh uniforms and not fresh mail bags?

She grinned mischievously. "You know what, Jack? I have something special just for you."

And there, on top of the stack of letters, was issue 150!

"Wahoo!"

I grabbed the stack of letters, but I couldn't take my eyes off my comic.

The front cover looked terrific - it showed Detective Gary trapped in a dark room, tied to a chair, surrounded by baddies.

But a thought hit me before I could get lost in my imagination.

"You know, Evelyn, you can just use the letterbox? You know what a letterbox is, don't you? I think that's important for a mail woman to know about."

She grinned at me, "Oh, haha, such a sassy boy."

I wasn't being sassy, I was trying to help her.

"I know about letterboxes, sweetie. But If I did that, we wouldn't get to have our little, *special* chats, would we?"

What's so *special* about them?

She continued, "Do you know what I think? I think you're probably the most incredible boy I've ever met!"

She stood there, smiled at me, tilting her head over to one side.

That was an *odd* thing to say.

That smile is *odd,* too.

She had only known me for two days.

But it felt kinda nice, anyway.

I wasn't really used to many compliments.

She placed her hand on the top of my head, and I instantly felt calm.

"…thanks."

She smiled at me again, saying nothing.

Staring.

Just for a few seconds, but I didn't like it much, just like I didn't like it yesterday either.

"Goodbye, Jack." Then she turned and walked away, so I shut the door.

Comic time!

After dropping the boring letters and things on the kitchen table, I ran up to my room with my comic.

I've been waiting so long for this moment, I could *hardly wait* to read it.

I know. I'll read it once now, and then again with the candy Mom's bringing back.

I hope it's a box of Mike and Ike! They're my favorite.

Whilst sitting all cozy on my bed, cross-legged, I opened the first page.

I was fizzing with excitement to start this new story, and then something fell out of the comic - *another* yellowish envelope flopped onto my lap.

Another one for fifty-two!

Evelyn!

This one was slightly larger and thicker than the letter from yesterday, like a birthday card, but still the same fancy yellowish paper and still the same strange handwriting.

Oh dear, poor Evelyn.

She really would get into trouble if the Post Office found out she misdelivered two things in two days.

I don't want her to lose her job.

I'll keep hold of this one with the other and talk to her about it tomorrow.

I looked out of the window at fifty-two.

Maybe it was someone's birthday soon or *something*?

I hope Evelyn can deliver these letters properly soon; I don't want them to miss their birthday card.

It was getting dark outside by the time Mom returned home.

She stunk of booze, cigarettes, and men's cologne… a lot of men's cologne.

She had been *working*.

Mom laid down on the couch and fell asleep instantly.

Oh… I guess she *forgot* the candy today.

I walked to the kitchen, poured my mom a glass of water, and put it next to the couch.

She works so hard.

That evening, I found myself something to eat for dinner, got ready for bed, and read my comic one last time.

It really was the best comic ever.

His escape was amazing!

Simple duct tape couldn't keep Detective Gary prisoner.

He says it's all about placing your fingertips together and trying to slap the wall behind you.

He's so smart.

Heroes *always* escape.

"Happy", I whispered to the air.

Then, I fell asleep with a smile on my face.

Day Three - The Package

Waking up in the morning was just like any other day during this July.

But last night I had an *amazing* dream where I was actually Detective Gary - solving crimes, being a hero and living like the coolest guy in town.

It was one of those dreams I didn't want to wake up from.

Actually, I guess today differed from other days - I had a mission to complete!

I needed to get Evelyn to take these two letters across the

road to fifty-two.

I got dressed and walked downstairs with the two envelopes and placed them on a side table near the front door.

It was really quiet downstairs.

Mom was nowhere to be seen.

I guess she already left for the day.

I didn't mind when she did that, although I missed our morning cuddles.

Not to worry, though.

I wonder what time Evelyn will be round today.

I hope it's soon because I think they're getting ready for the party at fifty-two - there were so many cars coming and going last night.

Probably getting the decorations and things ready, I guess.

Ding Dong

Walking towards the door, it was obviously Evelyn again.

I had gotten used to her outline through the frosted glass and even though I couldn't see any details through it.

I bet she was smiling long before I had even opened the door, though.

She probably is always smiling.

I opened it to the usual warm greeting.

"Hello sweetie. My favorite boy, Jack."

I *had* a mission.

I *needed* her to take these letters back.

I *wouldn't* get distracted.

"You need to take these." I held out the two letters to her.

"I think one is a birthday card and I would hate it if they didn't get their card. My Mom gets me hilarious cards for my birthday and I save them all. We are *fifty-three*, not fifty-two."

She carried on that smile and said, "Oh, Jack, I've already told you, they're for you to hold on to. I can't take them back."

"But…"

"It's our *little secret*, remember, Jack? My special boy."

The lavender smell from her was especially strong today and her uniform was as crisp as ever.

It looks fresh out of the packet, like she had only worn it for five minutes.

"Evelyn, you *need* to take them. You won't get in trouble. They'll just think the mail was late or something…"

She said, a tinge of disappointment in her voice. "Oh, Jack, I thought you were a big boy who was going to help me. But I guess I was wrong. I thought I could trust you."

"Hey, I'm *not* a kid. Take them!"

"NO… NO!" she yelled.

What was that?

I threw my hands up to my ears and covered them.

I hated loud noises.

"No, I'm sorry. No. I c-c-can't, Jack. Think of them as yours now. *All* yours. You must look after them." Her eyes were twitching ever so slightly when she said 'no.'

Then I noticed her picking the skin on her thumb with her forefinger.

Some kids in my class do that when they're anxious.

I guess she was really worried about losing her job.

But I don't like it when grown-ups shout at me.

This made me cross at Evelyn.

I was about to tell her that was fine when she turned and walked away, mumbling to herself.

Hey, she didn't even give me any post!

Why would she just ring the bell and not hand us any post?

I closed the door and tried to understand.

I *couldn't.*

Grown-ups are odd sometimes.

I went to the fridge and got myself an enormous glass of Sunny D, my favorite.

Wow, the fridge was cold; it made me *shiver.*

Just then, the doorbell went again.

I poked my head out of the kitchen at the front door but couldn't see anything through the frosted glass.

Odd.

Maybe the bell was being rubbish, and the button got stuck in or something? Making it go off by itself?

I went to the door and opened it slowly.

On the floor, in front of the door, was a small package.

It must have been about the size of my hand and wrapped in brown paper, tied together with string.

Like some really old-fashioned parcel used in black and white cartoons.

I guess Evelyn forgot to deliver something after all but was probably still too cross to hang around and talk with me.

I picked up the package.

Wow, it's *heavy.*

Good job I'm strong.

I turned the package over in my hand to examine the address.

Number fifty-two again!

What?!

That's it!

I stomped up the stairs with the package and the other letters and dropped them on my bed.

I'm going to open these stupid letters…

6th July

Dear Lucian,
The council has deemed your offer worthy. The local gift you
propose would be a most suitable match so we will send the artifact
in due course.
Please proceed with the preparations, get the gift ready, and we
shall summon the others.

D

A gift!

I knew there was a party happening!

That's probably what they're making preparations for.

That explains all the cars last night.

Oh no, Evelyn is going to mess up this person's party.

I better open the second letter and find out when the party is, there might still be time.

7th July

Dear Lucian,
If you are confident that the gift will be ready in time, we can
perform the rite during this cycle. Remember, the gift has to choose
to come to you freely.
I have enclosed the invitations we sent to other members.
D

A larger piece of card was in this envelope.

It was a *fancy* invitation card.

So, it wasn't a birthday card, but I was close!

It said that there's a gathering happening on 8th July at midnight at fifty-two Hill Drive.

That's tonight!

There is still time.

I bet the third thing, the package, is the gift they're talking about.

Although I don't know how it can choose to come freely, it's just a thing.

A heavy thing, but just a thing.

Anyway, what a fun mission this is turning out to be.

Detective Gary would be proud.

I'll be a hero!

I carefully opened the package, untying the string and unwrapping the crinkly brown paper.

The thing inside was a statue.

About the size of one of my mini action figures - six inches high, but it weighed an absolute ton.

The statue was green.

Like, really green.

Kinda like that horrible green and gray color of boogers I sometimes get.

The shape was a strange animal that looked like it belonged in the sea.

Its face was of an octopus, with long, thick tentacles hanging down from its mouth.

Creepy.

The thing was definitely not a real animal, though.

This thing had large bat-like wings wrapped around its back.

I definitely would have learned about an animal like this at school if it were real.

The statue looked old.

Really old.

Like it's been around for thousands of years or something.

Maybe it was an old action figure of some kind for the kid's party?

It would make an amazing comic book character - Detective Gary and his trusty sidekick Octopusman!

Just then, my mom returned home.

Drat!

There goes my chance of going across the road anytime soon.

I scooped the letters and Octopusman back under the bed and listened to hear if Mom was coming upstairs.

No footsteps.

I guess she's having a day in front of the TV.

I looked out of the window at fifty-two.

There were a few cars in the drive already and parked along the sidewalk.

It's definitely a party-day today.

I wonder how much work it takes to have a party.

Probably a lot, which is why I haven't had one yet.

Hopefully, one day, though.

Some cool-looking green lights were flashing up in the attic window.

Attic party!

That's got to be where the gathering is happening.

If I wait until Mom falls asleep, I should be able to sneak across the road, deliver Octopusman to the kid, wish them 'Happy Birthday' and get back before she notices.

Maybe I'll make a new friend whilst I'm at it.

A new friend would make the summer much more fun.

Accepting the Invitation

It was really dark by the time Mom fell asleep… now was my chance.

I put on my fluffiest, warmest bear hoodie.

Slid on my sneakers and crept to the stairs.

I was super sneaky, even though I didn't need to be. I could hear Mom snoring on the couch before I reached the bottom of the stairs.

I could be loud as an elephant, and she'd still not wake up.

Still, I carefully opened the door and snuck outside into the chilly fall night.

Brrr, it was *freezing*.

Colder than my fridge!

The cold cut through my hoodie, making me shiver.

Wow, the moon was big tonight. It looked slightly red too.

It made my mission feel even more heroic.

I realized I hadn't stepped outside the house for most of the week and the fresh air felt good.

My hot breath was billowing out in front of me.

I better get a move on.

Especially considering I had a critical mission to complete.

I looked up at the house and the green party lights from the attic were very noticeable against the dark night sky.

Those green lights looked exciting and made my heart beat faster.

"Here goes nothing…"

I crossed the quiet road and made my way towards the house.

Climbing the creaking, wooden stairs, I strode closer to the front door.

My initial plan was just to post the letters through the mailbox and put the statue on the doorstep.

Just like Evelyn had done to me.

Then ring the bell and run back home… but being outside was *exciting*.

Besides, if they were all gathered in the attic for their party, they wouldn't hear the doorbell.

Party music can be loud… I *think*.

So, if I did that, the kid would miss his present.

…Which was obviously *so important* as they wrote letters about it.

No, I would have to go in and deliver the letters myself.

Plus, that increased the chances of meeting the birthday kid and making a new friend.

I tried to open the front door, and to my surprise, it opened.

Probably so party guests can let themselves in.

I took one last look back at my house and then stepped into house number fifty-two.

Inside, it was spotless.

Way cleaner than my home.

No bottles or trash anywhere to be seen.

Everything is clean - like a doctor's waiting room.

Such a lovely smell too - was that? Lavender?

I like the smell of lavender. It smelled very… *familiar*.

"Hello?" I called out into the hall.

No response.

"Er… Hello. Is anyone down here?"

Still nothing.

All up at the party, I *suppose*.

Suddenly I felt scared to be out of my home.

This place felt really alien to me and I didn't want to get in trouble.

The quicker I delivered these letters and gave the gift, the quicker I can be back in bed with my comics.

I took a deep breath and climbed the stairs.

It took me a few steps before I realized that on the wall of the staircase there were paintings.

Lots of paintings.

Wow, they are weird looking.

Some showed stormy seas battering coastal towns.

Some showed strange looking families with funny faces - like that one disabled kid at my school.

They went all the way up the stairwell and around the landing, too.

Nearly at the top now.

I kept my head down.

The paintings made me feel really strange, so I didn't want to look anymore.

One painting caught my eye though - it looked a bit like Evelyn stood next to a man.

Actually, it looked JUST like Evelyn.

Hey, maybe that's why she cared about the letters so much? Her family live here or something?

Her relatives.

I could see the stairway to the attic now, just next to the painting, and it curved upwards.

Music!

I could hear music now.

And... *people*.

The sounds were coming from up in the attic, but it didn't sound like any party music I'd ever heard.

It was music, but also... *not music*.

It felt as if all the chords and notes of the song were being played in the wrong order.

I winced at the strange sound and thought about just dumping the letters here and turning back…

…but, after a few seconds…

…I felt *calm*.

Hidden in the screeches and odd clicks, a melody appeared.

So *beautiful*.

My feet started moving towards the stairs.

It didn't feel like I was walking, though.

My feet were carrying themselves up the stairs to the attic.

So *peaceful*.

So *magical*.

So… *hypnotizing*.

The door was open, and I walked into the room with the green light.

Inside the room, there were two rows of benches, with people dressed in black robes.

Under their hoods, I saw they were all wearing Octopusman masks.

It looked kind of funny.

But this didn't feel like a dress-up party.

Inside my body, deep inside, a small voice was yelling and telling me to run.

Run!

Run, Jack!

Run home and never come back!

But the music… so *soothing*. The music pushed that worry away and made me feel so calm.

At the far end of the room, there were two people wearing red robes, standing next to a large stone table.

Behind them, the entire wall was glowing green.

I called out to the room, "I... I brought your *gift*."

Then everything went black as I fell to the floor.

The Ritual

Ouch, my head.

It throbbed. Did someone hit me?

I woke, and...

Hey, why am I on the table?

And where's my hoodie?

The two red-robed people were talking in a funny language to the rest of the people.

I couldn't move my arms.

Someone tied them together with duct tape.

"Help me, please!".

A red-robed person turned and put their hand on my head.

A wave of calmness washed over me.

It felt... oddly familiar.

They removed their mask and smiled at me.

That creepy, enormous smile...

It was Evelyn.

"Oh Jack, you've done so well. We just need you to be a good boy for a little longer. We're almost finished."

"Evelyn? I... I don't *understand*...I..." I stammered.

"I said you were a *special* boy, Jack. The most special boy ever. Tonight, you'll see why."

She pointed at the green wall.

I turned my head and peered at the wall.

I cried…

It wasn't a cool laser effect for a party like I had first thought.

I could see *through* the wall.

Sort of…

It was like looking through a piece of green, frosted glass.

Just like my front door… but there wasn't a person on the other side.

But behind the glass, things *were* moving.

Large things.

Things like the tentacles of some giant octopus.

They were getting closer to the wall.

I looked back at Evelyn to ask what that thing was, but I couldn't.

She held a curvy dagger in her hand.

It made me scared, and I couldn't speak.

"You will be the first to meet him, Jack. My special boy. He has wanted to visit for so long and now you are the gift that can set him free."

She placed the strange statue on my stomach.

It glowed with the same bright green light as the wall…

…or *portal*, or whatever that was.

"The artifact with the blood of the gift is the key!"

The entire room erupted in that weird language again, all chanting the same thing over and over.

I remembered my mom, asleep on the couch.

Evelyn chanted something strange.

I remembered my house and my bed.

Evelyn stroked her dagger.

I remembered my comics.

Evelyn lifted the dagger above her head.

I looked down at my bindings. They felt like tentacles

wrapped around my wrist.

Evelyn closed her eyes, like in prayer.

"Heroes *always* escape..."

If Detective Gary can do it, then so can I...

I put my hands above my head, put my fingertips together, and threw my arms down with all my might.

Like I was slapping the table.

The duct tape snapped in two.

"Jack! No!"

Thanks, Gary.

I grabbed the strange statue on my tummy instinctively.

Wow, this thing was hot. It almost burned my hand.

I swung my left fist, holding the statue up at Evelyn as hard as I could.

It hit her, hard.

A mixture of teeth and blood shot out of Evelyn's mouth as she collapsed onto the floor with a muffled moan.

The chanting from the others carried on.

They wanted to finish whatever it was they started.

But the other person in the red robe turned, grabbed the curvy knife, and jumped at me, sticking it into my tummy.

I screamed.

Red-hot, burning pain shot up from my stomach.

A spray of red blood filled the air as he removed the knife.

I screamed like a *little boy*.

Blood flowed out of my stomach and onto the table, sinking into grooves and channels.

As my blood ran down the groove towards the wall, the green became more see through.

Like I was *opening the way*.

"Yes. It is working. Just a few more seconds..."

Still holding the statue, I threw it at the man's head.

It crashed into his face with a crunch, and he toppled back.

I dropped the statue.

I swung my legs over the table.

And sprinted for the stairs.

As I ran, the people in the robes carried on chanting.

They were still trying to cast the spell.

When I reached the door, I looked back and saw a huge tentacle, almost the width of the entire wall was right at the green glass now.

A wave of fear and terror came over me.

That's *not* an octopus.

That's a… I don't even know *what* it is.

It looked *ancient* and *powerful*.

As I stared at the creature, I did a little boy thing.

I wet myself.

I never felt so scared before.

Then, something else caught my eye.

In the room's corner, crumpled up in a heap….

…was Harry.

Naked Harry.

Dead Harry.

I gasped, turned and sprinted down the stairs.

Reaching the front door, I flung it open and forgot about the stairs at the front.

I fell all the way down and landed on my back.

I looked up at the house and heard the chanting from inside change.

Instead of all talking in some strange alien language, they were now all screaming.

And the screams were very much in English.

Screams.
Lots of screams and squelches.
And then, the green light was gone, and it was all quiet.
I shuffled backwards, stood up, and ran back to my house.
My Mom was still on the couch, so I ran and jumped on her.
I love my mom so much.
She saw that I was bleeding and called 911.
I just wanted to fall asleep in my mom's arms…

Dreams

It's been a few weeks since that night.
I don't dream of Detective Gary anymore.
I only dream of 'it'.
People keep trying to ask me how I got so bloody, why I was outside, or if I saw what happened across the road.
Something or someone killed everyone, they say.
The police say that someone broke in and attacked the people at fifty-two and he must have attacked me too.
But I know *what* killed them.
I saw it.
And it wasn't *people,* or a *person…* it was that *thing.*
And I still see it…
Every night in my dreams it's there.
The ancient, giant tentacled thing.
They all keep saying that I was a *lucky little boy*.
I don't feel *lucky.*
But I won't tell them anything.
I can't speak.

The words won't come.

Anyway, even if I could, who would listen to me?

After all.

...I'm *just* a kid.

The Ancient One Below

14th December 1242

We have found it… In the name of the Lord, amen; we have found it.

On the 4th day of this month, brothers Thierry de Nuss, Rembald de Voczon and myself, Jacques de Montreal, discovered that most unholy place deep within the Carpathian Mountains and unearthed a relic that defies all knowledge but is obviously holy in nature.

This campaign in the Burzenland has seen us Knight Templar engage many Mongol warriors over the last few years, who seem intent on conquering the known world, but what we found on this quest into the mountains was not defended, nor, I would guess, known by any Mongol warrior. Instead, unknown warriors dressed in the blackest of robes guarded that place and seemed to worship some religion or deity that my brothers and I could not comprehend. They spoke a language most strange that chilled the three of us equally. Heretics, the lot of them.

Still, upon engaging us in combat, they were no match for

our heavier armor and superior tactics, yet they came at us with such fervor, almost throwing themselves onto our swords. By God, the three of us cut them all down without so much as a scratch on our shields. Brother Rembald himself dispatching five alone and myself four. As the unholy zealots lay dead on the floor, their blood still dripping from our longswords, we opened the large double doors, of which they guarded so desperately, and realized this crusade was worth the ten-day trek. For inside we found an artifact. A relic. A vessel?

My brothers and I have yet to identify the object but can feel the power it emanates. The relic emits a glow and an audible hum when held. A gift from God indeed. Its small size, fitting perfectly in two cupped hands, contrasted with the chamber where it lay: a room truly gargantuan in size. When we first entered that vast, inhospitable place, we saw the relic atop an ancient, raised altar in the middle of the room. It seemed the altar had been there for centuries, as though the entire temple was constructed around it. You may imagine that this was the most shocking object in the room, but my brother you would be wrong, for to get to the altar we had to cross a grated hatch in the floor, the circumference of an entire fortress. The pale green mist covering the bottom of the pit, visible through the hatch, prevented us from seeing its full depth, but the way in which it echoed our footsteps, it was obviously incredibly cavernous. Whilst walking over the grate, Brother Rembald became violently sick; gripped by some fever or illness and fell to the floor. Perhaps a reaction from the fighting that came before? Perhaps by some fumes venting up from below? To further add more mystery to that fateful day, Brother Thierry was convinced he had heard something down in the mist when he bent down to help his ailing brother. However, I believe he was simply letting his imagination run wild. Staring down into such an incomprehensible void, such as he was, I feel it somewhat justifiable that his mind could wander, considering the unnatural surroundings we three found ourselves in - how can the mind fathom such a place even exist?

We secured the artifact and began our climb back outside, up the stone carved staircase to the entrance some three hundred feet above. As I climbed the stairs, I felt the object getting heavier… perhaps it was simply time for my imagination to play tricks on me, much like it had for my two brothers. Thinking back, it seems strange to me that such individuals guarded such a relic. Was it worth their lives?

Upon resurfacing from that dank, defiled, underground temple, and back out into the snow-covered mountainside, we were greeted by a most disturbing sight. Our mounts were thrashing around in such a fit of panic and fear at our sight that we were lucky they didn't break free of their hitching. We calmed them just enough to secure the relic to the pack on my horse and began our ride back to Dietrichstein fortress. We barely spoke whilst riding or when we made camp at night. Brother Thierry especially seemed to be affected by the entire ordeal and violently woke each night on the journey home, claiming to have seen something hideous in his dreams. No doubt due to the sheer depth at which he peered through that grate. Now that we have returned, I hope a feather bed tonight will help, and he can shake this affliction of the mind for good.

However, as I write to you now, the wooden walls of the fortress seem to offer little immediate comfort for the three of us. We can not help but wonder…What have we discovered? What was that hatch sealing deep below? Who were the robed figures and to which god did they serve? We shall continue to investigate, and I will write again when we have made some progress. But first, we must sleep. I long to put the whole thing behind me and focus on the relic. God wanted us to find it, of that I am sure.

It is the strangest thing, but the horses seem restless still and have been these ten days past since we retrieved the artifact. Hopefully, a good night in the stable with other horses will calm their mood.

May you perceive this letter and may the God of peace be with you all, dearest brothers.

Jacques de Montreal
Knight Templar

16th December 1242

This relic, I fear, defies God himself. After spending an entire day studying the thing, I am convinced this is indeed a gift from God… just perhaps not our God. The power that resides inside calls to me, and I often find myself staring at it for an unknown length of time. I feel powerless to resist its lure and fear the devil could be at work here. The other brothers argue against it, but in order to know our enemy, we must study it. I must examine it. I must hold it. Touch it. Feel it.

…No! Curse this sinful desire. We are servants of God and I will not be turned. I will continue my studies with the utmost will.

The artifact has writing on it, but I cannot identify the language. I consider myself a learned man; I have a bookcase full of tomes, but yet this language has me confused. If anything, it shows that there is a lot more to learn of this world, both past and present, and I will dedicate my life to find the answers - in the name of God.

Brothers Rembald and Thierry both continue to suffer in their own ways. Rembald continues to be violently sick, whilst Thierry's mind continues to deteriorate. They are both being cared for and all our prayers are with them. They are strong men, they will pull through.

Meanwhile, the horses continue to be afflicted by some addling of the mind that we cannot fathom. They have started to kick at the stable door at night, longing for freedom, but there is nothing outside our walls other than snow and rock. I am sure they will settle soon.

Glory of God to you all, dearest brothers. We stand as one.
Jacques de Montreal
Knight Templar

17th December 1242

Dearest brothers, we must be steadfast in our faith, for the devil does not sleep. We are stronger than him, for he knows that if he tries to persuade you to sin, you will not listen and will not consent. The other brothers here in the fortress are of the belief that this artifact is of the devil's design. But I am not so certain. I do not think someone so evil could create such a thing of beauty. However, is it not an example of how the devil can work? The invisible enemy who is always tempting and cruelly pursuing. He strives to spoil the good work which you are performing with proper and rational zeal. As his aim is to spoil the action by corrupting your intentions, when you kill, he suggests that you do it out of hatred and rage. When you take plunder, he suggests that you are doing so out of greed.

It is not greed that has allowed us to obtain this relic. I believe we have liberated it from the clutches of those heretics in the defiled temple. I am still studying, day and night, but I am growing more certain that those robed figures had stumbled across the artifact by chance, were in awe of its power and beauty and built a new religion around it. Or perhaps resurrected an older religion... an ancient one, devoted to some deity who they believe to be older than time. Something down in the depths of the world. Something that lay sleeping. Waiting.

How do I come up with such a theory? There is only one true God, so why does my mind slip to such fancies as imagining an elder being down below, manipulating the men above to do its bidding? Surely my mind is just imagining that decrepit pit in that temple, wondering who would need such a large entrance. It truly was beyond belief.

The artifact itself continues to amaze. Not only is it an object of absolute beauty - its sharp pointy corners and unknown ornate relief, which covers the surface, continues to pose more questions than answers. Its power is still very apparent, though. Touching it still gives off an audible hum, yet there are no clockwork mechanisms at work. How is it generating power? And to what purpose?

I discovered something even more astonishing this morning; the artifact seems to influence things around it as well. Upon waking, I was shocked to find the artifact had pulled all the other items on my desk towards it. Either that, or one of the other brothers was in here, trying to touch the relic. I wish they would leave me alone. It is mine to study.

Thierry has now started having waking visions of …things. He claims to have visions of two giant eyes down in the fog beneath the temple. Large, bulbous eyes, long black tentacles and a body covered in pustules and boils. A truly horrific sight, I can imagine. Rest is best for him. For his safety, we have locked him in his quarters. Pray for him.

As for Brother Rembald, he seems to have shaken his nausea he first encountered in the temple. I can finally no longer hear him vomiting day and night. Praise be to God. I know the horses have especially perturbed him at night, breaking what little sleep he can find with their constant cries and panicked thrashing around. Normally such a patient brother, I fear the illness and the combat against the heretics have caused his faith to wear thin. Peace, brother. I hope he finds comfort in his own studies whilst we are here. The horses will settle soon.

Peace to all.
Jacques de Montreal
Knight Templar

18th December 1242

The horses are dead. They went mad and ate one another. The neighs, whinnies, and screams echoed throughout the cold, frost-bitten fortress last night. Their wide, blunt teeth snapping through their own flesh, which was a sight straight from hell. No-one got any sleep. Brother Rembald could not bear the sounds any more and dispatched a few with his own sword. A kindness, I am sure. At least we will all sleep better tonight. Although, how we will leave this snow covered fortress without our mounts is another problem. Why would we want to leave, though? The relic is here. We need to stay here to care for it.

My studies offer little sleep for me myself. If I sleep, I can no longer look at the relic and I so want to look at the relic. Always.

Brother Thierry spends the day wailing, convinced some unholy force is marching upon Dietrichstein, drawn to the relic itself. He says he has seen a giant, ancient, being in his dreams - telling him to open the gate. Nonsense. I have told him we are safe, but more importantly, the relic is safe within our these walls. My words offer him little rest, but I do not doubt there is something powerful happening here. I swear it though, if any being, malevolent or otherwise, attempts to take the relic, I will defend it with my life and with God at my side, no-one will touch it.

My studies continue. Nothing else matters.

God is great and we are his servants.

Jacques de Montreal
Knight Templar

20th December 1242

I have locked the door, sealing us in the room, the relic and I. My relic. Mine to study and mine to protect. What happens outside this room is simply insignificant, as this room is my universe. It is THE universe. God has commanded me to stay here. He talks to me through the relic. He… he tells me things. Shows me truths.

Brothers, I weep as I write this, as God has chosen me to be the protector of the relic - to keep it safe until he can arrive to claim it. We will see him soon, I am sure of it. I will be ready.

He will be here any day…

God is peace.
Jacques de Montreal
Knight Templar

21st December 1242

The time has come. There is fighting outside the fortress walls. I hear the death cries of my fellow brothers and the growls of their enemy. As I write, it has become clear to me as to the origin of those sounds - they must be angels - champions of the true God. My God.

He has sent angels ahead to pave the way to the relic. Obviously, they have deemed the others in this wooden fortress to be lesser beings and are summarily judging them as we speak.

I do not know how many of my brothers remain alive. Few, I would wager. If I have to continue my work alone, then I shall. I think I have been alone for days, but can one truly be alone when sitting with a relic from God? He will reward me for my work by lifting me up.

When I am summoned, I will open the gate and let him in, just like he has asked me to.

GOD IN PIECES.
Jacques

22nd December 1242

He is here.

The fighting has stopped.

Everyone but Thierry is dead. I hear him frantically scratching around.

I care not. My God is here.

I will go to him now…

I can feel him call to me.

He is ancient; he has come from below.

Taller than any living thing, older than time itself.

The true God. My God. God of everything.

Thierry has set fire to the walls. The flames have trapped us in.

I won't stop him.

We don't need our physical bodies anymore.

Fire will not kill us.

Goodbye mortal realm, I ascend now.

Ggggoooooodddbd
Jacwques
Kihyngt

15th April 1245

Dear all who may read this,

The Dietrichstein fortress burned down in 1242, along with Jacques de Montreal and my other brothers of the Knights Templar. Locals are unclear why or how, and historians should forever remain puzzled. The order will say its destruction was at the hands of the Mongols. This is good. We must keep these enclosed letters safe; no one must know the truth of that place.

I will leave this land and return home. I have seen and heard things that will forever change me, yet my faith remains unshaken, because I believe it was faith that gave me the courage to overcome those monsters and that thing.

The thing... words will not be enough to describe its gargantuan appearance. I do not think as a species we have the vocabulary for such a sight. I have no doubt it was an Elder God from a time long before and I am convinced it will forever haunt my waking moments. God gave me the strength to escape from my locked room and discover that fire was enough to drive it, and its unholy hoard of minions, back into the mountains, but I did not defeat it, not fully, for I fear it is merely sleeping. Waiting...

As for the relic, the fire was enough to stop that devil from reaching it. However, I know not where it lays now. Buried deep under the wreckage, I should guess, and hopefully shall remain forever more.

I have sealed the entrance to the temple. It is imperative that the ancient one must not awaken again.

By all things holy and good.
Thierry de Nuss
Knights Templar

4th December 2024

To: TommyG1123xrp@hotmail.co.uk
Subject: Check this out. Find of the century!

Body: Hey Tom, I can't believe what I've stumbled across. These are real life letters by Knights Templar that I found hidden in one of the archives!

They talk about Dietrichstein fortress!! Fucking Dietrichstein fortress!!! Do you know what that is? That's the wooden fortress that burned down in Transylvania. Well, it wasn't called Transylvania back then, but after it burned down, they built Bran castle! You know that one, I'm sure. It's the castle that was in the inspiration for Bram Stoker's Dracula. No-one knew how the wooden fortress burned down... except now they do, because I FOUND IT!

Sorry, I'm really bloody excited (if you can't tell). Reply to this email and let me know when we can meet. I have to show someone the original letters, otherwise I might explode.

Your passport is up to date, right? Fancy a trip to Romania? I bet we can find that sealed entrance and/or the relic… we're gonna be famous.

P.S. bring a shovel.

Steve,

Truth Seeker at www.TemplarHunter.co.uk
The truth is ours to find. We just have to look.

The Vengeance of Lilith Thorn

Lilith stood at the edge of the old wood and gazed across the boggy waste that had once been a lush, fertile farm. Past the bog and fields of blight, in the village that she had called 'home' for so many years, the few remaining victims faced their inevitable end. Sickening screams, gargling breaths and panicked cries filled the night air as her cracked, dry lips twisted upwards into a sickening smile. She knew it was *her* magic that had caused all this suffering and death.

Her power.

But all of it, from the rotten crops that lay right in front of her to the foul smell of bloated, pestilence-ridden corpses wafting across the bog on the winter night's breeze, was justified.

THIS was the vengeance of Lilith Thorn…

…and it was all made possible because of *him.*

Lilith wasn't always this way, far from it. Growing up, she was a good-mannered child, although her life wasn't without struggle. She was born and raised in the village as a sixth daughter of six, with the village mayor as her father, and found it hard to form meaningful connections with her peers. Whether that was because her father was the mayor, or how she preferred the company of animals to people, she didn't know, but the other kids of the village teased her. So, when she wasn't being bullied in school or performing her chores at home, Lilith would often go out to seek solace in the nearby wood. It was here where she discovered peace, for there were no cruel taunts from the trees or nasty jibes by the various critters of the wood. But they *did* talk. Lilith was sure of it. And what they said was *beautiful*.

Others in the village didn't understand. One time, a cruel girl from her class caught Lilith with her hand on an old oak, giggling at an unspoken joke. The other girl informed the school, which then spread like the plague, as often gossip does, to the entire village, leading to Lilith being taunted and labeled "a witch." At first it was a joke, at Lilith's expense, but as the vicious taunts grew louder, it forced Lilith into that wood, her place of solitude, even more and before long she was spending more time with the trees and animal folk than at her home. This irked her sisters as they were the ones who had to explain to father and pick up her abandoned chores.

"Lilith? Lilith Thorn!" Yelled John Thorn, her exasperated father. "Where is that blasted daughter of mine this time?"

"Father, please. Can't you see she needs to be alone from time to time?" replied Alice, the oldest sister. "Just let her be… for once."

"From 'time to time'? 'Let her be'? She spends so much time in that blasted wood it's no wonder she doesn't grow fur and live up a tree. I won't have it! The gossip has become too loud, Alice." John said as he rubbed his face in despair, "I want you to go to those woods and get her back. DRAG her back if you must, but I will have a woman made of her. She's thirteen on the morrow!"

"…yes, father, but if only you could…"

The conversation ended abruptly, as there was some sort

of commotion happening outside the town hall. John rushed outside to witness the entire village in an uproar. Lilith was being carried around the square, naked and covered in bramble scratches - paraded like a deer recently shot on a hunt. Every villager was there, or so it seemed, and was enjoying the spectacle. John stood and watched as they laughed and hit her with sticks, as they shouted "Witch!". They caught her *cavorting with dryads and treefolk*, they said. *'Speaking in tongues'*, another alleged.

All lies.

Of course, there was a trial, and the mayor tried his best to cover up the whole thing, but the village folk wouldn't let the matter drop.

They wanted this troubled girl *silent*.

They wanted her *to go*.

They wanted her... *Dead*.

The villagers were blaming Lilith for *all* their recent misfortunes, from crop failure to sickness and fertility rates. Everyone knew the punishment for witchcraft was burning at the stake, but by the grace of her father, Lilith was allowed to live, but he, too, secretly wanted her gone from this place. So, he used his mayor status and exiled her. Banished her from the village, never to return. Lilith left the people behind and walked to the one place she felt safe, the one area to provide comfort - the wood.

Lilith knew of an abandoned hut there, only a mile or so from the village's edge. It probably belonged to an ex-woodsman as it had a rickety wooden bed, overturned log as a table, and a *mostly* functioning roof. She'd sometimes visit the hut when she truly wanted to be alone.

Except she was never alone.

Not *really*.

As she walked out of the village for the last time, she knew the hut in the wood would soon be her new home and she smiled. She felt… happy.

No more expectations.

No more people.

Just her and nature.

Lilith *was* good. She knew it deep within. She wished no misery on anyone, no matter how hard they hit or how much they spat. Although, this time, something was *different*. Being cast out by her father while her sisters did nothing - her own *flesh and blood* - changed Lilith. It had planted a metaphorical seed in her chest. Just a small one, but it would soon grow and blossom into something spectacular.

She made a functioning life for herself at the hut - gathering berries and mushrooms to eat, which were abundant in the wood, and drinking from the fresh streams that provided life to so many. Lilith was always good with nature, always felt happy whenever she was around it. Happier than others. She had a bond with it. Some latent *power* that quietly called to her. She would spend every day tending to the world outside her hut and would surround herself with nature all day until nightfall.

However, at night, *always* at night, she'd wonder… *things*.

Ask herself questions.

Dark questions.

So, over time, the small seed inside her… *grew*.

How could they blame her for the failing crops or for the lack of rainfall? Surely the farm hands who tended the crops had more to do with it than she? So why did they spit at her and call her names? What had she done to them to warrant such bile? It wasn't fair. She would have done anything to fix the troubles of the village, even though she knew nothing of farming. They called her 'witch', but if she were a witch, she would have used her 'magic' to save the village, not curse it.

She would have saved them all if she could.

Then, one dark and stormy night, a few months after the exile, when the village had probably forgotten all about Lilith Thorn, a thought bubbled up from within, as she lay in bed… a thought from the *seed*.

"…*would* I save them, though?"

The doubt that had been slowly building from within, over time, combined with her natural primal power, was enough to call forth *him*. He came to her for the first time that very night…

Lilith… Lilith. Hear me.

"Who's there?" Lilith startled, sitting bolt upright in her bed.

It is me.
Thou hast called me.
I am the Old One.

She looked around her dark hut, lit only by the moonlight. There was *something* inside with her, but she couldn't quite focus on it. She turned her head left and right, trying to identify the visitor.

"I-I can't see you, but I know you're there," she called out into the darkness.

I am here. I am always here.
Always on the periphery of vision.
Always but a whisper in the ear.

Lilith trembled, "…S-Satan?"

No. I am older. Far older.
From a time before humans walked. Before religion.
I was here before the beginning and will be here long
after the end.

Lilith felt her body quivering. "What do you want with me?"

You are special.
I can make you…
More.

Lilith stayed quiet. This voice, this being, was a stranger in her sacred space of the hut, but she felt a strange familiarity for him. Like a long-forgotten friend.

After a while she stopped trying to look for this being, hung her head and just accepted his presence.

Then, he asked her three questions…

Does thou want solitude?

"Yes."

Does thou want power?

"…yes."

Does thou want... Vengeance?

Lilith paused. She did. She knew she did, and this scared her. Why should the village carry on as normal, as if she never existed? Why should they continue to blame others for their own problems? Now that Lilith had gone, they'd surely turn on another innocent girl within the village to punish. She shuddered at the thought. No, they *needed* to learn the error of their ways. They needed to *repent*.

"Yes!" she exclaimed into the darkness of her hut.

Then it shall be so.

With a crack of thunder, the Old One was gone, and something entered Lilith. Within an instant, she could feel *everything*. The energy in her own body seemed to pulse. A growing power inside her, a dormant power that had always been present but was now unlocked by the pact with the Old One, surged into life.

She stumbled out of the hut, into the rain-soaked night, and she laughed such a laugh. She *felt* the very life-force of the earth beneath her toes; it flowed like a river up through the soles of her feet. She could *see* the heartbeat of every woodland animal, *hear* the song of every flower and *understand* the trees as they whispered to one another. She felt connected to everything. Lilith cut short her laugh and snapped her head toward the village.

"They call me 'Witch', so I will be that witch. They will pay."

Lilith felt... *thirsty.* But not for water. This thirst was for vengeance. Pure and primal. The pact had caused the seed inside her to grow into a sapling, and it needed sustenance.

She knew how to quell the thirst - she'd lay a curse on their farmland. She pictured the crops in the village farm, closed her eyes, imagined the hatred the villagers had for her, felt the lash of the brambles on her skin. Then, an ancient word somehow found its way up to her lips. Lilith closed her eyes and spoke it, sending the spell out into the world.

Lilith's body crumpled over, clutching her knees with both arms, but not from pain.

"What…what *is* this?" Lilith whispered to herself.

Then, like stepping into a hot bath on a cold winter's night, a warm feeling grew from within until it completely covered her.

It was… joy.

Bliss.

Elation.

The unbridled ecstasy that throbbed from the tips of her toes to the end of her dark hair was unlike anything she had ever experienced. She never wanted this feeling to end. She stumbled back into the hut, smiling, and lay on her bed. Lilith wanted to be at one with this feeling. To be one with nature. And so, she closed her eyes and drifted off into a long sleep.

Time passed. How much time Lilith didn't know, but it didn't matter. Time didn't seem so important anymore, but it must have been a few weeks considering the growth of the surrounding plants. She sat up in bed and felt… empty. That joyous feeling had subsided.

Could it all have just been a dream? A strange imagination brought on by a fever or a cold, perhaps? No, she felt a stronger connection to the surrounding nature than before. She was sure of it. Lilith stood up from the bed, feeling refreshed, invigorated, and noticed how the floor was full of berries, nuts, and mushrooms. The denizens of the wood must have come to her whilst she slept, bringing gifts. Lilith was always kind to the critters of the wood, and now they thanked her with offerings. She nodded her head, gave her thanks and walked out of the hut towards the village.

On the walk, Lilith questioned her actions and her dealings with the Old One. Had some demon of the old world tricked her? Had someone or *something* played on her naive nature or her apparent loneliness? No. The Old One wasn't a demon. Lilith was sure of it. He was a god before man even knew that gods could exist. An ancient god of nature and she was lucky to have communed with him.

She felt no guilt for her part in what happened that night and knew that if the curse was successful and the crops failed, she'd feel no remorse and she could go about her life with this vengeance sated.

When Lilith reached the edge of the wood and looked out upon the village, she couldn't believe her eyes. What was once an enormous field of wheat, corn and vegetables was now a fetid bog. Sulphuric steam rose from the puddles that twinged her nostrils.

Lilith smiled. She had delivered the vengeance.

She turned and went to walk back to the hut when something pulled at her.

A tug on her soul stopped her in her tracks.

She knew, instantly, that it was *him.*

This wasn't enough. The village deserved more. They could just grow more crops, so what lesson or vengeance have they actually received? Lilith thought about the beatings she endured. Surely, they should feel some physical form of vengeance too, right?

"No," Lilith whispered to herself, her forehead furrowing into a deep scowl. "They deserve *more!*"

She snapped her heels together, turned to face the village again, and grimaced with hatred. She fell to her knees, thrust her fist down into the earth and *screamed!* In the distance, she could see villagers rush around the village square, trying to find the source of the noise, but it was too late. The curse, planted in the soil, spread slowly under the ground, towards the villagers. Soon it would inflict the first of many by the way of a deadly, unprecedented pestilence.

Lilith rocked backwards onto her back and thrashed around in the grass with pure bliss. That feeling was back. Her thirst disappeared.

"Yes!" she cried as she thrust her hands out to her sides, grabbing two fistfuls of dirt. "Oh, yes!"

It felt stronger this time, more intense. The sapling inside her had grown into a tree now. She felt as if her power was unlimited, she could do anything and no-one could stop her. The world was hers.

"More, I want more!" Lilith thrashed around on the floor, writhing and laughing, until sundown. As the village slept and an exasperated coughing fit echoed from the village square, she returned to her hut to rest.

The curse was deadly. Lilith would return over the course of a few weeks to witness the villagers fall one by one to the pestilence. Just as their vile gossip and lies spread through the village, so too did Lilith's plague. Skin bubbled and pus-filled boils erupted, spreading the sickness even quicker. Rats came and fed upon the deceased, but Lilith's curse didn't harm the animals, just the vile, cruel humans. The rats just wanted to help.

Lilith Thorn's vengeance was almost complete.

Once the disease had run its course, she returned to the edge of the village one last time. She wanted to see the results of her work. Her lips cracked as she smiled, for she knew the entire village was in their last few hours of life.

She had one more word for the village.

The *last* word.

A powerful word that would send every remaining villager tumbling to the floor with blood streaming from their eyes. And so it was. For the handful of people left, it was a quick death.

Far quicker than they deserved.

And then there was... *silence.*

No more humans here to blight this land.

Overtime, nature would reclaim the village, and everything would be as it should be. As she stood, trembling from the pleasure of it all, *he* came to her one more time, at the edge of her sight.

My Lilith.
You have served me well, but there is more to do.
More human blight to scrub clean from our Earth.

"What would you have me do?" Lilith casually asked. "Where shall I deliver our vengeance next? Let me taste more of your power."

And you shall...
There is another village just over the hill.
Deliver your vengeance to the human filth there.

Lilith grinned, now a dark servant of nature and the Old One.

Addicted to the power thrust upon her from her ancient ally, she turned and skipped towards the next village, with a special word already on the tip of her tongue…

Stranger at the Station

He's still staring at me…

It's been nearly 2 hours, and he hasn't moved from that bench. Arms crossed, black coat, long hair, massive black boots. He looks so damn creepy in this light. At least, I *think* he's staring at me.

Geez, what's wrong with my brain? Maybe he's thinking *I'm* staring at *him*? Haha, it's obviously just someone waiting for a train as well, and my mind is playing tricks on me. To be honest, the way the moonlight is reflecting off his glasses, who's to say that he's even got his eyes open?! He probably went to a Christmas party in town, had too many eggnogs and has fallen asleep waiting for his connecting train.

…Or maybe he's dead.

Shit, does that mean I need to wake him up? I'm not going over there. No way!

It'll be sod's law that the second I cross the bridge, my train will come, and I'll have to run back across and I really don't want to miss the last train.

I just wanna get back to my bed. Anyway, I'd break my ankles trying to run in these things - gorgeous as they are, these heels are not built for a life or death survival situation.

I hate the forest. Why does Sean have to live so far out in the countryside, anyway? We're city folk and always will be… at least I thought we were. Still, Sean was so chuffed to hang out this evening. I think he's finding it tough being out of the city now that Dad's gone. Although Dad would roll in his grave if he saw his only son living out in the sticks. He'd probably call him a 'country bumpkin'.

I miss ya, Dad. You'd sort this guy out for me.

Crap, he moved! He's not asleep! That's good, right? Well, I suppose it means he's not dead at least.

But… that means his eyes *are* open.

So, he *is* looking at me.

Why?

"Elo luv, cold night, innit?" he called across the train tracks. I almost shat myself.

"Err, yeah, good evening," I replied. Right, pleasantries done. Now leave me the fuck alone, please. I tried to convey that message without actually telling him to fuck off. If he is a crazy psycho killer, hell bent on murdering me and dumping my body in the woods, the last thing I wanna do is upset him.

The Stranger lent forward, and even though it was still a good 10 meters away, and over the other side of the tracks, it felt like he was invading my personal space. Like he was leaning in to give me a kiss or something. Why won't he just fuck off already? I'm not interested.

I'm not gonna look at him anymore. I don't want to give him the wrong idea. It's like the setting for the world's worst rom-com - an older gent locking eyes with an eighteen-year-old blonde, heading back to uni from visiting her brother and they cuddle up on a bench for warmth before making love in the snow.

Yuck.

Thanks for that image, brain.

Time to check my phone again… great, still zero bars. Why is there never any goddamn signal out here? You'd figure there are enough satellites and shit whizzing around up there to give enough coverage for the entire country. Wait… is he rubbing his leg? Oh god, he *is* a pervert. Fuck off, old man. Get the hint already.

It's only ten minutes until my train, but I don't know if I can do this… he's still rubbing the inside of his leg and staring. Stop fucking staring! Oh god, if he stands up I'm out of here. Why can't I just have a normal night? Why do creeps always come and find me? I mean, I guess he could have a sore leg from sitting on that metal bench… but what's more likely? Sore leg, or super horny from looking at my gorgeous face? Definitely the latter. I have that effect on weirdos.

"This is a customer announcement. The 11:35 train from Southampton Central has been canceled. Please see the timetable for alternate connections. We are sorry for any inconvenience caused to your journey."

He's getting up! That must have been his train! He's coming over here!! Oh god, oh god. No! He's gonna kill me! He's walking up the steps now. I need to move; I need to not be here. His hand is in his coat. Is he getting a knife? I bet he is!

Nope. I'm not staying on this platform and getting stabbed.

Five miles isn't that far…I can walk.

Fuck walking, I'm going to run. Sayonara, you creep! Peace out!

CRACK

ARGH, fuck! My ankle. GOD DAMN IT!

Geez… I don't think it's broken, but I'm not stopping to

check… I'm too scared to look behind me. This country lane seems to go on forever.

No, I need to check if he's coming for me; I need to know.

OK, here goes nothing…

I turn my head…

Is..is he following me?

The Final Log

"Hello? **Gzzzzt** C-can anyone hear me?" The radio buzzed to life, punctuated with bursts of ear-splitting static, like nails down a chalkboard.

Nicole Hooper jolted awake, lifted her head, and rubbed her eyes. Why was she on the floor?

"**Gzzztttt** Commander? Anyone?" The voice on the radio sounded more panicked now.

Hooper pushed off and floated over to the other side of the module, fumbled for the transmit button and replied, "Jones, is that you? What happened?"

"Hooper? Oh my god, is that you? Geez, I thought I was the only one left. You OK?"

Hooper tentatively touched her forehead and felt a giant bump forming. "I hit my head pretty hard. But I think I'm alright. How about you? Everyone else OK?" Hooper asked.

"Yeah, I'm good. The station seems to be intact, with no obvious damage. I haven't heard from the Commander or Vasili yet though…" Jones trailed off. "Hoops, what the hell was that thing? Did you see it?"

"No, what do you mean?" Hooper replied. She hated being called *hoops*. It reminded her of school. "I just heard an explosion and then the lights went out."

Hooper raised her hand up to a large bump on her forehead. "Gah, my head is killing me!" She muttered to herself, making sure her thumb wasn't on the transmit button. When she pulled her hand away, she noticed it was trembling uncontrollably. Shock.

"Oh right… Yeah," Jones said. "It's just…"

"*Gzzzzt* Jones, Vasili, Hooper. Sit-rep. What are we dealing with?" The voice on the radio was stern and authoritative. "Anyone there? This is Commander Mackenzie. Report!"

"Commander! Thank God!" Jones replied over the radio. "Me and the botanist are OK. No word on our mission specialist, though. The station seems to have sustained zero damage, which I suppose is one good thing going for us."

"Great. Jones, see if you can find Vasili and let's all meet at the cupola." Mackenzie ordered. "I need to see what happened with my own eyes."

"This wasn't exactly the type of first contact we had imagined, huh?" Jones said, his voice quivering with a tinge of uncertainty.

"Look, we need to get our bearings," Mackenzie said, ignoring the *first contact* statement. "You have your orders."

"What if…" Jones hesitated, genuine emotion showing through his jokey facade. "W-what if it comes back?"

There was silence on the radio.

Hooper knew Jones would still be there, clinging onto the radio, waiting for some sort of response from the commander. But she also knew that the commander would already be on his way to the cupola by now. However, she couldn't leave him hanging…

"Come on, Jones," Hooper calmly said. "We don't know anything yet. Let's just go meet the commander. You remember what he always says? 'Assess fully and THEN react'. Get Vasili and I'll see ya there."

Hooper carefully secured the radio against the Velcro fastening, let go of the wall, and glided over to a small mirror on the other side of the module, where she checked herself over for any cuts or grazes - nothing. Good. Getting a cut in zero gravity would be *problematic*. Sure, the bump on her forehead looked like a real shiner, but at least there was no blood. That was something. She took a deep breath and made her way to the observation module - the Cupola.

It had been a few weeks since Nicole Hooper had arrived on the ISS, and she still wasn't used to the zero-g environment. As she pulled herself through the tight, white corridors, full of beeping lights and expensive looking computers, she was always super nervous of accidentally bashing into some important piece of tech. To say that she and technology didn't get along would be an understatement. She was a botanist - an 'outdoors gal' who liked nothing more than tending to a garden. Wherever that might be - a garden in a backyard, on a rooftop, in a lab, but soon she'd be cycling down onto the moon to join the lunar team with a large container of seeds, vegetables and plants. A garden on the moon!

The commander, however, was practically a veteran already and knew, with utmost importance, the need to keep his shit together for the sake of the crew. However, deep down in the pit of his stomach, Mackenzie knew this situation was FUBAR. After so many missions, you just had a knack for knowing when crap has hit the fan.

When Hooper arrived at the cupola, the commander, Jones and Vasili were already there. Jones with his head in his hands, Mackenzie darting from window to window and Vasili staring dumbfounded into nothingness.

"It's *gone…*" Vasili whispered.

"What? What's gone?" Hooper said in utter shock.

"The Moon. The fucking moon isn't there!" Jones cried.

"What are you talking about? How can it just vanish!?" Hooper exclaimed. She felt the urge to laugh. This was obviously a big joke… Right?

"We've must have been spun around!" Mackenzie barked. "Each of you take a window!"

Seeing the urgency in which Commander Mackenzie spoke sent a chill down Hooper's back. This was real.

Hooper glided past and looked for herself.

Nothing.

Where was it?

How could it disappear?

The four astronauts looked out of each window and then checked the computers to make sure they hadn't rotated or moved. Nope, same orientation as before, but it was true. The moon was nowhere to be seen. What could have happened? Surely if it had exploded or something, there would be debris everywhere?

But there was nothing.

Absolutely nothing.

Just the endless void of space.

As if the moon never existed in the first place.

After his initial outburst, Mackenzie's training kicked in immediately and he knew he had to contact Houston. "I'm going to contact mission control. They'll know what to do." Time seemed to flow in slow-motion as the commander floated across the room, towards the radio.

"Houston, this is Commander Mackenzie of the ISS. Do you

read me?"

"*Ggzzzzztttttttt*"

Mackenzie tried again, "Houston. Do you read me? This is Commander Mackenzie of the International Space Station. We're requesting a sit-rep. Everything OK down there?"

"*Ggzzztttttttt*" More static.

"It's no good. I already tried." Vasili explained. "It's just us for now."

Mackenzie slammed the radio down.

Hooper floated in silence - confused by what was happening. She felt lost, cut off, and alone. Her head was spinning. If there was no moon, why was she even up here? Her big break at NASA seemed to have vanished, just like that. Her brain couldn't process the madness. However, she was glad Vasili was around. Out of the four of them, Andrei Vasili was always the calm one.

They were alone.

"The radio's down? How is that even possible?" Jones snapped. "Surely our satellites are still functioning? Hell, I can even see them out the window! So why can't we fucking contact Earth?"

"Jones, calm down," Mackenzie said, straightening up. "There's always a rational explanation. Maybe whatever caused our blast sent out some EMP blast or something and temporary fried the satellites?"

"...But didn't affect *our station*?" Jones retorted, getting more and more irate. "Excuse me, commander, but that doesn't make a lot of sense does it?"

"Well, maybe the blast did something to ground-control? We don't know, so stop assuming. It's not helping the current situation!" Mackenzie barked, before taking a deep breath to calm his nerves. He needed to hold it together for Jones' sake, but that man always had a way of getting under his skin.

"Err… Commander," Vasili interrupted, "with the moon gone, what will that do the people down there? Surely it can't be good?"

The four looked down at the huge planet. From here, everything looked totally normal down on Earth. Tranquil and beautiful as always - the big blue marble. But with the radio down, how could they know? The four astronauts all sat in silence. They knew full well what would happen down there without the effect of the moon, and it won't be good.

Mackenzie remembered what Jones said earlier and snapped out of his stupor, "Hey, Jones, you said you saw something? Explain to me what it was. What hit us?"

Hooper turned her gaze towards Jones. She too was wondering what the hell it was he thought he saw.

Jones suddenly remembered the vision of it, the thought hitting him like a truck. "I don't think anything hit us, commander. But what I saw was big. Like, *really* big."

"What? Like a meteor passing by?" Hooper wondered, clutching at straws, trying to help.

"Do meteors have tentacles? Do meteors have eyes?! No, it wasn't a fucking ball of ice, Hoops!"

Mackenzie shot him a look.

Jones took a deep breath. "Sorry, Nicole. Look, I don't know what it was… I've never seen anything like it. I hope it was just my mind playing tricks on me."

"*Eyes*? *Tentacles*? Really, Jones?" Mackenzie said, eyebrow raised. "Do me a favor and keep the overactive imagination in check, please."

"Wha.." Jones wanted to snap back before Vasili turned,

sensing this conflict was about to spiral, and interrupted. He knew the commander and Jones had a tendency to bicker, so said in his calm Russian accent, "What about the Luna mission? The crew down there would have seen everything. We will have all their audio logs."

The four of them floated in the same stunned silence after that sentence.

Down there.

Down *where?*

Where exactly were they now? There was no moon left!

The Luna mission had a team of astronauts stationed on the moon for a few weeks as they constructed a permanent habitat for future, longer trips. It was the job of the ISS to provide support, if required, and to monitor their progress. Hooper herself was due to go down there in a few days to prep the site for agriculture work. So, what was going to happen now? What the hell had happened to the Luna mission? Surely, they would have had a front-row seat to whatever transpired? He understood that their survival chances were pretty low. However, this gave Mackenzie something to focus on, and something to distract from the nonsense that Jones was shouting.

"Yes! Good idea. Let's go check the comms log," Commander Mackenzie ordered, exerting a comforting level of authority for his crew. "I'm sure that will shed some light on this situation, and we can get a bit of clarity back. Lead on, team." Hooper led the way and floated down and out of the observation pod, towards the comms croom, being extra cautious to not bash into any of the equipment in front of the commander.

The four moved silently through the station, trying to process the madness of what they just saw. Or didn't see. But this wasn't the first time Mackenzie and Jones had been in a tough scrape. They met twenty years ago, back in the Air Force, and forged a lasting friendship. However, they were prone to the odd clash here or there. Mackenzie was a disciplined pilot and rose quickly through the ranks, earning a reputation for his strategic thinking and decisive leadership. Whilst Jones was a charismatic but impulsive crew member, often acting on emotion rather than logic. During one fateful training mission, Jones' recklessness led them to bypass protocol and attempt a dangerous aerial stunt. The aircraft malfunctioned, and they ejected behind enemy lines, sending the F35 crashing into a mountain. It was only because of Mackenzie's quick thinking and survival instincts that the pair got through enemy territory undetected. They escaped with their lives, but the incident resulted in disciplinary action. Jones struggled with guilt and anger whilst Mackenzie grappled with the ramifications of his choices on his career. However, both atoned for their error and eventually joined NASA to become well respected astronauts. He needed him then, and he needed him now.

Vasili, on the other hand, kept himself to himself, so no-one really understood his past escapades, but he definitely gave the vibe of someone who's seen some shit.

But how can they use their experience to navigate the fact that the moon had vanished? There was no protocol for that. They all tried to examine the evidence and provide a rational explanation. Maybe something knocked the ISS off course, and the moon was on the other side of Earth? No, that was nonsense - the readings confirmed it. The station was still in the same location as always, floating 408km above the Earth. They were clutching at straws, trying to think of a concise, rational explanation to explain the last crazy few minutes.

However, Jones saw *something*.

He saw... *it*.

So, whilst the others were trying to think of a solution, he couldn't stop picturing the vastness of what he saw. His mind couldn't process the image, as if it were trying to shield him. He couldn't find the words to describe it, but how could he when what he saw was so... *Infinite*.

Vasili, the mission specialist, in charge of communications for this mission, calmly found the recordings of the last few hours and got them prepped for playback. He turned to Mackenzie, which snapped Jones out of his existential dread, and said, "Here we go, Commander."

Mackenzie took a deep breath. "So... Let's see what our friends saw. Play the logs."

Not knowing what they were going to hear, and with a sense of hesitation, Vasili reached forward and tapped the 'play' button.

Start Transmission

Hughes: *Another day on this beautiful space rock.*

Palmer: *Amen, brother.*

Hughes: *Hey, at least we're on course to get the O2 generator up and running for the habitat today.*

Palmer: *Good! Will that mean we might actually get to take these damned helmets off? I hate these fishbowls.*

Rhodes: *Keep it professional guys. We've got a job to do.*

Palmer: *Easy for you to say. You get to sit with your feet up back on the shuttle whilst me and my boy Hughes are out here doing all the hard work.*

Hughes: Very true! That reminds me, we need to talk about our contracts. We thought we deserve a raise.

Palmer: That's right!

Hughes: ... well, seeing how we do all the work out here.

Rhodes: *sigh* America's finest engineers, right here. The taxpayers will be proud! Just get on with it, we can discuss your remuneration when we're back home... and let's keep chatter to a minimum. For my sake.

Hughes: Hey, when's that botanist joining us down here?

Palmer: In a couple of days, I think. Why, are you bored of me already?

Hughes: Why though? Even if we get this 02 genny up today, we're not gonna have a breathable atmosphere for ages.

Palmer: She's bringing down some stuff to prep the area. Ya know, to get the site read first... I think she's also coming with a cargo of seeds and stuff as well for later.

Rhodes: Guys! Get to work!

Palmer: Fine. Right, let's get cracking. Hey, pass me the...

Hughes: ... er, guys, are you seeing what I'm seeing?

Palmer: Where? Oh geez, what in god's name is that?

Hughes: Oh. My. God.

Palmer: Looks like the aurora borealis...but in space! It's gorgeous. Look at all the colors - purple, blue, green... Wow.

Hughes: ... I-I don't like it!

Palmer: Rhodes, you seeing this? It's some sort of mirage, right? Some distortion because of space dust, or *something? I'm right, aren't I? Erm, Rhodes?*

Rhodes: *... I ... I'm getting some funny readings here ...*

Palmer: *I know I'm right. I read about these fancy space effects. Like fireworks going off in space because of rays from the sun.*

Hughes: *Geez Palmer, can you shut the hell up?! You're not a scientist. Rhodes, what is this?*

Rhodes: *... get... g-get back to the shuttle. Quick!*

Palmer: *Relax, it's the biggest firework show in the galaxy and we got front row seats.*

Rhodes: *GET BACK NOW! THAT'S AN ORDER.*

Hughes: *... something is coming out of it.*

Palmer: *... what is that?*

Hughes: *It's... a tentacle!? It's m-multiple tentacles.*

Palmer: *Look at the size of them. They've got to be twenty thousand miles long!*

Hughes: *Geez. That body! It kinda looks like a cephalopod.*

Palmer: *Those eyes must be as big as the whole of Europe. Geez. What is it!? What THE FUCK IS IT?!*

Rhodes: *Commander Mackenzie, you guys seeing this up on the ISS? This is Commander Rhodes from Luna Habitat team, requesting help...*

Hughes: *Rhodes! Screw the ISS, contact EARTH dammit!*

Rhodes: *Right. Er, Houston, this is Commander Rhodes of the Luna Habitat team. We have discovered first contact with an unknown entity in space. It appears to have entered our solar system by the way of some sort of gateway. My guess is that it's a portal of some sort. Can you confirm?*

Rhodes: .... *Houston. Do you copy? Is anyone there?*

Palmer: ... *Please, help us.*

Hughes: *Aliens!? It can't be an alien. It's too big!*

Rhodes: *Team, back in the shuttle. It's turning. It's... It's coming this way!*

Hughes: *Where's the little green men? And the flying saucers?*

Palmer: *I can't do this. I can't do this. I can't do this.*

Hughes: *Palmer, get it together. I'm here. We'll be OK.*

Palmer: *No no no no no no. Not like this.*

Hughes: *Palmer, stop flapping at your helmet. ... NO! Get your hands off your helmet. STOP YOU FUCKING IDIOT.*

Rhodes: *Hughes, what's happening? My monitor is flashing like the fourth of July, it's saying Palmer is unfastening his helmet? Stop him!*

Hughes: *I can't reach him! Shit, no, Palmer. STOP! NO!*

Palmer: *This is on my own terms... ARRGGH.*

Hughes: *PALMERRRRRR!*

Palmer: *...................*

Rhodes: *Team!? Report!*

Hughes: ... *he's gone. I-I couldn't stop him.*

Rhodes: *Oh, Palmer...*

Hughes: ... *he always hated that helmet, the stupid fool!*

Rhodes: ...

Hughes: *Rhodes...*

Rhodes: *Yes, buddy?*

Hughes: ... *It's coming for us, isn't it?*

Rhodes: *It would appear so. Yes.*

__Hughes__: All our damned hard work... for nothing! We were so close as well to getting off this rock.

__Rhodes__: Maybe it'll pass us by?

__Hughes__: Oh god, I think not. It's looking right at us and floating this way. Its mouth is opening.

__Rhodes__: Mouth? Fuck me. This is it then. I'm glad I can't see it from here... but at least it'll be quick, buddy.

__Hughes__: The devourer of worlds...

__Rhodes__: You know what's funny? I thought we'd be famous for this mission. I thought I'd be giving talks in schools to my grand-kids and their friends...

__Hughes__: Well, put it this way, we are going to go down in history for being the first humans inside an alien squid thing. Oh god, the ground is shaking...

*__Rhodes__: I'm going to try mission control and the ISS again. Houston and Commander Mackenzie, I don't know if you guys are receiving this, but this is a mayday. Palmer is deceased, suicide, and Hughes and I are about to follow. The entity is about to consume the moon. Geez, what an absolute bonkers statement to say! *sigh* I suppose this is the moment where I should try to say something poignant, something to go down in human history, but all I can think of is my wife. Tell her I love her and let her know..........*

End Transmission

The four crew members sat in silence, stunned at what they just heard on the audio log. You couldn't exactly hear a pin drop because of the soft hum of the various computers, but the silence seemed to go on for an eternity.

That was until Ryan 'Jonesy' Jones broke the silence with an exasperated tone and said, "The moon was fucking *eaten*?!"

The absurdity of it all. Not only had the Luna Habitat team allegedly discovered alien life, but it also devoured them, moon and all. Surely not! However, the crew couldn't argue with the facts. The moon HAD disappeared; the audio logs WERE genuine and Jones HAD seen something.

Remembering that Jones said he witnessed the entity, Commander Mackenzie sprang into action mode. "Right. Jones, explain to me exactly what you saw!" He was going to leadership the hell out of this situation. "I want a full verbal report, followed by a written one on my desk first thing tomorrow."

"You don't have a desk." Vasili calmly clarified, without looking up from his console.

"You know what I mean!" Mackenzie snapped back. "We can't salvage this situation if we don't know what we're up against."

Jones' face dropped, remembering the horror he glanced at from the window in his quarters. "It was big."

"Yes. You said that already," Hooper chipped in. "The Luna team mentioned it being twenty thousand miles long or something. Was it THAT big?"

"Erm, sure. I mean, it could have been."

"Maybe it was something that skimmed by us really close. And it looked big?" Vasili wondered.

"Jones, describe it. In detail!" Mackenzie pulled out a small pad of paper and pen from his suit.

"Well… as well as being big, it had these long tendril *things* which looked like they were coming out of its face." Jones swallowed, his mouth dry. "Can I get a drink or something? Might calm my nerves a bit."

"Vasili," Mackenzie gestured over to her Russian crew mate. "Could you get Jonesy some water, please?"

Vasili nodded and floated out towards the kitchen.

"Continue…" Mackenzie was trying to piece all this together. "So, the *thing* had a face?"

"It did. Yeah…"

"Did you see how it appeared? The Luna team talked about an 'aurora borealis in space'. Did you see anything like that? A wormhole or gateway?" Mackenzie thought this was an important fact, as the entity and 'portal' weren't out there now. So maybe the thing went back through.

"Erm, I do remember thinking it looked like space had shattered. Like someone had thrown a rock through a greenhouse window." Jones said, shaking his head in disbelief. "Is that what you mean, Commander?"

"Hmm mmm" mumbled Mackenzie as he scribbled in his notebook.

"Guys, maybe that's what caused the earthquake feeling in here?" Hooper said, remembering the violent shaking and gently prodding the lump on her forehead.

"Anything else? Please think," asked the commander.

"I'm not sure I want to remember anything else, Commander. It hurts," Jones said, whilst rubbing his face. "I *do* remember that it had these two enormous eyes, though, like dark voids. It sounds weird to say… but they were strangely *beautiful*. When I looked into them, I swear they looked back. It saw me and in that moment I think I saw… I saw…"

"Go on…" the commander encouraged.

"The end."

"End of what?" Hooper leaned in closer.

"*…all things.*"

The three floated in silence again, contemplating what that meant. Was Jones being overly emotional or dramatic again, or did this being telepathically show him the end of days? The hums of the computers around the module seemed slightly more oppressive now.

Just then, Vasili floated back into the comms room with a bottle of water, which made the trio jump out of their skin - Like children telling a spooky story around a campfire.

"Jesus, Vasili. Can't you knock or something?" Exclaimed Hooper, who startled the most, dropping her pen, which now just hung in place.

"… but there's no door to knock," Vasili replied, obviously confused by English sayings.

Mackenzie gave Vasili a firm look before focusing his attention back on Jones. "Right, let me confirm this then… a large entity, with long tendrils, two void-like eyes, appeared from some sort of hole in space, destroyed the moon and then vanished. Is that all we have to go on?"

"Its mouth." Vasili added nonchalantly.

"Huh?" Jones questioned.

"It didn't destroy moon. It consumed moon. Luna team say it had mouth and you cannot consume without mouth." Vasili was a very matter-of-fact man.

"God, he's right." Mackenzie tucked the notepad back into his suit.

"But why? Why would something want to eat the moon?!" Hooper asked in disbelief. "It's just a big gray rock. Maybe to consume the minerals or something?"

"I have been thinking about this," Vasili began. "Humans

wanted to build habitat on moon. Branching out into space. If alien race were watching, they'd not be happy." Vasili's English, whilst somewhat broken, was doing a great job of conveying his theory. "When humans are just on Earth, they are no threat. When others realize they can colonize other planets, they are threat. End the threat before it has chance to *be* threat."

"…I think he could be on to something. We have always assumed aliens would be little green men - humanoid, roughly our size. This thing is very much *ALIEN*. It really is a 'devourer of worlds', isn't it?" Hooper said.

"So, we're not alone in the universe," Jones said, shuddering as he spoke. "It makes you wonder, what else is out there? Is this an alien or a monster or just a space beast? It doesn't make a lot of sense."

"I think we have to assume it's an alien, Jones," Hooper said. "It's alien, by the dictionary definition. It's not supposed to make a lot of sense. It's *alien*."

Mackenzie floated in silence as his crew around him discussed aliens, space beasts and first contact. What was happening? He needed to get a grip on this situation again.

"So, what if alien comes back?" Vasili was thinking practically. "How can Earth fend off such a colossus? We are nothing but ants."

"… maybe it's a god?" Jones wistfully wondered.

"OK, right, Jones… it's *not* a God," Mackenzie rubbed his face. "This is becoming a problem. You need to cut out the crap, ASAP. We all just need to keep it together and get back to work! Vasili, I want you to try to contact the Luna Team… or Houston… or anybody, for that matter. You're the mission specialist in charge of comms, right? So, get a line of communication up somewhere, dammit! Jones, do another check of the station to make sure there really is zero damage and keep that mouth and imagination of yours in check. And, Hooper, carry on prepping your seeds and samples for your trip down to the moon in a few days. We're professionals, so let's get to it!"

The three being given orders glanced from one to the other, not quite knowing what was happening. Was the commander just in denial? Did he really think the moon was still there somewhere? How could they carry on with their regular jobs after something like this? Everything felt so trivial now. How do you even place yourself in the universe after this, let alone perform chores about the station?

WHOOP WHOOP WHOOP Suddenly, a proximity alarm sounded from every speaker in the station.

"Hold on to something, brace for impact!" Mackenzie ordered.

"It's happening again!" Hooper yelled as she grabbed onto the nearest solid object.

The station rocked from the force of a giant wormhole opening nearby - the massive fluctuations in gravity caused every bolt and panel of the ISS to quiver and bulk. Intense vibrations and jolts sent anything that wasn't fastened down, scattering through the zero gravity environment. The four astronauts clung on and managed to ride out the storm, which pleased Hooper. She wasn't sure her head could take another beating like last time. When the station stopped quivering, Mackenzie ordered everyone to fasten down all the loose items and then directed the team up to the Cupola for a better look.

Like kids peering through an enclosure at a zoo, looking for the elusive animal, the four took different windows and scanned the vastness of space.

"Do you see it? Do you see the thing?" Jones was quivering as he spoke, almost excitedly.

"Nothing here," Mackenzie said.

"Nothing here, either," Acknowledged Vasili as he floated over to another window in the observation pod.

"Maybe it was nothing?" Hooper wondered.

"Let's hope so, Hooper," Mackenzie replied. He was getting scared, but he'd be damned if he admitted that or showed any fearful emotion to the crew. "We're going to be OK."

"… Commander. You wanna know something?" Jones asked.

"Sure."

"I kinda wanna see it. Properly I mean."

"You were almost crapping yourself earlier," Vasili commented.

"I know, I know. But like… it's an alien! Don't you want to see more of it too?" Jones asked.

"No. I do not." Vasili ended the conversation with his abrupt tone.

After a few moments, Hooper tried to align with Vasili and said, "Vasili is right, Jones. If this thing wiped out the moon because it didn't want humanity spreading out into the stars, then who's to say it's going to stop there? Why not just get rid of Earth entirely and be done with it? No. It's much better than it hasn't returned. I think we're going to be OK." Hooper was trying to reassure herself as much as her crew.

For a few seconds, the four felt a slight calmness returning. They couldn't see it, it wasn't here! Maybe the vibrations and the proximity warnings were because of some sort of other space event, like a solar flare or something. But then, just as the adrenaline was fading from the initial scare, Vasili spotted something.

"...great," Vasili sarcastically whispered. "It's back."

Vasili saw the similar distortion in space as described by the Luna Habitat crew - A violent rupture in the fabric of space itself rippling with iridescent colors. Then, from the center of the disturbance, the *thing* swam through...

It was a planet-sized abomination, a god of nightmares, floating silently into the solar system. Even when only it was partially through the portal, the team could see its grotesque, almost incomprehensible form. A vast, undulating mass, with tendrils stretching like living rivers from what could only be called its *face*. And its eyes... those eyes. Two impossibly large, glowing voids flickered around in the sockets, searching for *something*. As it floated fully through the portal, it blotted out the sun and stars, and the four could finally understand its gargantuan size. A wave of nausea washed over Mackenzie. There was simply no training for something like this.

"...Look at the size of it," Hooper said. "They were right. It IS cephalopodan, but also *not* at the same time. Like a weird fusion of flesh and void. I've never seen anything like it."

"I don't think anyone has," replied Vasili.

The head, an unfathomably vast, undulating distorted mass, which bore the vague resemblance of an ancient, abyssal squid turned towards Earth. Its writhing tangle of tentacles coiled, stretched and reached across space. Some tapered into delicate filaments, whilst others were as thick as mountains, enough to wrap around... planets.

"Commander, I think thing is going for Earth!" Vasili exclaimed.

"I... I should try contacting them again," Mackenzie said, stunned at what he was seeing. However, her body wouldn't move. It *couldn't* move. Only stare...

"COMMANDER!" Vasili prompted again.

Commander Mackenzie shook her head free of the monstrous visage and floated over to the radio on the wall. He picked it up and froze. "…What in God's name should I say?!"

"Look at it move… it's beautiful," Jones said under his breath, unblinking at the monstrosity. A small smile forming in the corner of his mouth.

Its skin was a deep, unnatural hue. Something between obsidian and the deepest violet, speckled with bio-luminescent patterns, that shifted and undulated over its entire body. With each movement, it seemed to distort the surrounding space. Almost bending the void. It was too much to fathom. Too ancient and too alien for the human mind to comprehend.

Mackenzie slammed his thumb on the transmit button. "Houston, this is Commander Mackenzie of the ISS. I don't know if you're able to receive this, but a large, alien entity has entered our solar system and appears to be heading towards Earth. Houston, do you read me?"

Nothing.

They were alone.

They could only watch.

Not only did the alien entity defy all logical explanation, it also posed another horrific problem for Mackenzie. He prided himself on knowing a counter to every problem - a solution for every scenario - but this was a problem that he didn't have *any* training for. No-one had training for this. How could they? There simply wasn't anything in the playbook for something of this magnitude, and it caused him to feel incredibly useless.

He *was* useless.

Tears formed in the corners of his eyes as he grappled with that thought.

The thing circled around the Earth, slowly, patiently, as if studying its prey. The four astronauts could only imagine what the humans would be seeing down there. Would there be panicking in the streets? Phone calls to loved ones? Military leaders scrambling to do...*something?* But what could humanity really do? If it were an alien invasion out of the movies, they'd have heard a rousing speech, scrambled the fighter jets and attacked the flying saucers in the atmosphere - yelling something about "shooting green stuff" and then they'd destroy the alien mother-ship with a USB stick. However, this was too much for humanity to comprehend and plan for.

Too ancient.

Too alien.

Too final.

When you can't even make sense of something when you look at it with your own eyes, how can a species even strategize a defense? Especially against something so humongous that it would have its own gravitational pull. The four astronauts knew it would have been wreaking havoc down below.

The vast, eldritch colossus made Earth look like a marble in its presence and now it wanted to feed.

"I can't believe we're not alone in the universe..." Mackenzie muttered, barely louder than a whisper. "I...I don't know if I can do this."

The two, void like eyes, locked onto Earth and each giant tendril shot down towards the planet.

The tentacles coiled around the Earth, wrapping the planet in an inescapable embrace.

"No, please. Just leave us alone!" Commander Mackenzie pleaded into the radio, speaking on behalf of his species in sheer desperation, his once professional demeanor completely evaporating.

They watched as continents shattered like fragile glass. The very crust buckled and split apart, magma pouring from the wounds like blood. The atmosphere burned away in mere moments, reduced to ghostly wisps in the vacuum.

And then... it *pulled*.

"We are witnessing the end of days, my friends," Vasili said, resigned to the fact that was it.

"Amazing..." Jones gushed. "Isn't it amazing?"

The Earth trembled violently as it was torn from its orbit. The four watched in helpless terror as the creature's tentacles pulled their home, their entire world, and everyone they loved towards its humongous abyssal maw.

A massive, gaping orifice beneath its writhing face held thousands of spiraling, jagged ridges, the size of mountains, that could have been teeth, or something far worse. It swallowed slowly, deliberately, savoring the crunch of continents, the succulent taste of ocean and the implosion of the molten core.

Then, after only a few seconds, the Earth vanished into its depths.

The blue planet was gone.

Only silence remained.

The thing just floated, motionless, digesting its latest conquest.

The four floated in silence.

"It's gone..." Hooper whispered. "All those people..."

"It would have been quick death," Vasili said, trying to provide some comfort. "There's nothing anyone could have done."

"Wasn't there? You sure about that?" Hooper wiped the tears from her cheeks. "Maybe if we used our resources on our home planet better instead of *needing* to branch out to other planetary bodies to colonize. To live. To *infect*. Like a virulent space plague, which would have spread again and again. This alien was just the medicine. To kill the disease before it spreads too far."

"It did its job," Vasili sighed.

"…and it was the most beautiful thing I've ever seen," Jones said, his mouth wide open in awe.

Jones' ridiculous statement snapped Mackenzie back into life, "What the hell, Jones, what are you on about?! We've lost everything!"

Jones laughed, his mind utterly wracked with the incomprehensible vision before him. "It showed me this. It really was the end of days… it blessed me. It chose me to witness," Jones said, still transfixed by the alien's eye.

Hooper turned to Jones and yelled, "Jones! What the hell…" She stopped mid-sentence, staring at Jones' face "…y-your eyes. What have you done?"

Blood was escaping from Jones' eye sockets and floating in the air. Like his body was trying to draw out the poison of what he had seen. He looked too long; lingering in the void.

"I've… seen the darkness," Jones said, still staring at the thing's colossal, motionless, void-like eyes. "The eldritch one has gifted me."

"You've seen the darkness? What are you on about?!" Mackenzie said, his face grimacing at the sight of all the blood hanging in the air.

"You're scaring me," Hooper cried. "Commander, what's happened to him?"

"*Everything* has happened to me. It is more than an alien. It is a god. An ancient one from *before* and I am part of it now…"

"OK, Jones, buddy," Hooper tried using a calmer voice. "How

about we go down to med-bay and you let me look at those wounds?"

"Don't you see it? Don't you see the vastness of the void?!" Jones was cackling as he spoke.

"Geez, you're not making any sense," Hooper said. "Come on, let's get you down to the med-bay."

"I can't do this," mumbled Commander Mackenzie as he turned and floated away.

"Commander? What the hell, come back!" Hooper cried after him.

"I saw what lies beneath the stars. I saw it see me." Jones lifted his two bloody hands in the air as he spoke. "It's still looking... It *never* stops."

"Ignore the commander. Grab Jones," Vasili said to Hooper.

Hooper thrust out a hand to pull Jones away from the gaze, but as soon as she grabbed his shoulder he flopped backwards, like a rag-doll hanging there in zero g.

As he spun backwards he giggled, blood pouring out his mouth where he had bit his own tongue, "...it has me now."

With those final few words, Jones passed out and floated back into Hooper's arms.

"Vasili, quick, help me get Jones down to med-bay. He's sick," Hooper said, her voice quivered with panic.

"Come," Vasili said and began to lead Hooper to the med-bay.

Vasili, normally so calm and assured, floated in complete silence. However, having an internal problem within the ISS felt strangely *comforting*. For a moment, it took away from the existential dread that lingered outside the station. They were here. Inside the ISS, they had their own little bubble to focus on.

Hooper assessed the situation. "I think it's psychological,

but we need to check him over and try to stop this blood loss." Blood was still seeping out and in the zero gravity environment it looked like red, sticky ribbons, slapping into the normally sterile white panels.

"Yes, boss." Vasili floated ahead towards the med bay to prep.

Boss? Why did Vasili default to thinking Hooper was now in charge? Did he yearn for a leader that much?

Moving Jones through the tight corridors was surprisingly easy. Hooper tried hard to focus on the here and now, refusing to look out any of the windows she passed. She felt that if she didn't look, she didn't have to acknowledge the thing. Out of sight, out of mind. She reached the med-bay, got Jones set up on the table and strapped him down, securely. "Oh no, Vasili, look at his eyes!"

Vasili leaned down for a closer look. "They look like... claw marks".

"Did he... claw his own eyes? His eyes look fucked." Hooper inspected closer. "These look like... fingernail scratches. My god, it *is* self inflicted."

"He won't see again," Vasili said, in his matter-of-fact tone, again.

"... sorry Jones," Hooper said as she stroked Jones' hair. She looked around and grabbed the suture kit. "Let's get him stitched up and stop this bleeding, at least. Then we'll look at his tongue. The damned fool."

Vasili administered a strong sedative to make sure Jones was in a dreamless sleep, so Hooper could operate.

The two worked in silence, fixing up their crewmate as best as they could, both too afraid to voice the thought they shared. If they voiced it, they'd have to face it, and neither wanted to do that. Such existential dread is simply beyond the human brain's capacity.

"He won't be pretty, but at least he isn't gonna bleed out now," Hooper said as she finished up the last of the suture work. Then, out of no-where, Vasili said it…

"Why are we bothering, Hooper?"

It's true. Why *were* they?

Humanity was lost.

The planet consumed.

Surely, everything was futile.

Why did it matter if Jones lived or died? Why did it matter if he was going to be 'pretty' or not? Nothing mattered. Everything was pointless. Why carry on?

Hooper straightened up, carefully putting away her medical equipment, and barked, "We bother because we CAN! Because we DAMN WELL CAN!" Hooper slammed her fists on the table. "We will NOT just give up and roll over, regardless of what that hideous thing out there thinks! We are humans, DAMN IT, and I refuse to accept that this is it. I have family back on Earth and I want to go home…OK?!"

Vasili floated, dumbfounded. "Yes, Nicole."

"Great!" Hooper sighed. "Thank you. I'm sorry. Look, I'm glad you're here with me."

The two shared a quiet moment together, with just the soft hums of the machinery piercing the silence.

"Now that Jones is stabilized, how about we find where the Commander got to? Give us something to do," Hooper asked. "You check the quarters and…"

Suddenly, Jones snapped upright on the bed, snapped through the restraints, his mouth wide open, and let out a terrifying, inhuman scream, "AEEEEEEEEEE!"

Hooper couldn't believe what she was seeing. He should have

been completely out, from the sedative. The sound was unlike anything she had ever heard. It sent shudders down her spine and bored its way into her brain. She floated, dumbfounded by what she was witnessing, not knowing what to do.

Vasili, calm as ever, reacted immediately and floated over to the table, and grabbed Jones by the shoulders and attempted to secure him back down onto the table.

Jones reached up, clamped his bloody palms on Vasili's face and, whilst squeezing like a vise, pulled his head closer so they were nose to nose, then whispered, "Join me in the darkness. Join me at the end of all things…" and with a sickening crunch, Jones violently twisted and snapped Vasili's neck.

"JONES, NO! STOP! WHAT ARE YOU DOING?! OH GOD, VASILI?" Hooper cried out, but it was too late. Vasili's body hung there, motionless, as Jones discarded him like a used toy. This wasn't Jones, though. It was Jones' body, sure, but this wasn't him. She had to get out of this room.

Hooper pushed against the ceiling and propelled herself towards the hatch to the next module. This was pure fight or flight, and her body had chosen the latter for her. She didn't know where she was fleeing to, but she just needed some distance between that thing and herself so she could assess. Assess the threat and *then* react. Just like the training that Mackenzie kept going on about.

Hooper floated all the way to the far end of the station, the engineering module, and slammed her back against the far wall - staring at the hatchway she entered from and began counting, fully expecting Jones to come gliding towards her at any moment.

Ten.

Nine.

Eight.
Nothing…
Six.
Five.
Four.
Get a grip, Nicole.
Two
One.
Adrenaline flooded her quivering body.

She finally let out a breath. It was ragged and tense. She wasn't cut out for this, she just wanted to grow flowers for god's sake!

Just then, an arm floated down onto her shoulder.

"Fuck!" She yelled, as she spun around.

It was the lifeless body of Commander Mackenzie with a screwdriver buried into his temple. His right hand still gripped the makeshift suicide weapon.

"Oh, Commander… *Why?*" Hooper whispered, covering her mouth to stifle any involuntary sound that might escape, giving her position away. But she knew why. Of course she did. How could she blame him?

She didn't have time to mourn; she reached up, unclasped Mackenzie's grip on the screwdriver and yanked it out of his head. A line of blood licked across Hooper's face causing her to gag slightly. She pushed Mackenzie's body away and then marveled at the sheer futility of this situation.

"Oh god. Seriously, what is the point of this? Of any of this?" Hooper exclaimed out loud. What a perfectly accurate snapshot of humanity this whole situation was. There were four people left in the whole of the species and they were trying to kill each other or themselves. It was here, in this moment, that Hooper accepted her fate and went to look out of a window at the thing.

It still hung there, completely motionless, in the space that Earth once inhabited. Like a piranha, just waiting for the next scent of blood. Jones had been right about one thing though; it was strangely beautiful to look at. Jones… Oh, Jones. She couldn't leave him in this state, a husk of his former self, acting on behalf of the thing out there. If he was still in that body somewhere, she needed to do something. She needed to set him free. With an inner resolve, Hooper said, "I've gotcha, Jones. I'll make it quick." Then she tightened the grip on her weapon and pushed off towards the med-bay.

Up ahead, Hooper heard horrific screams mixed with the violent smashing of equipment. Those screams also sounded… *alien.* So inhuman. She could use this as a distraction, though. His focus on the computers would keep him from focusing on her. Then, after an enormous bang, the lights of the station went out. Descending Hooper and the thing formally known as Jones into pitch black darkness…

"RAAGGHH!" Jones roared in the distance.

Hooper hung, completely motionless, in the dark. Waiting… waiting…

Vooooom The station's backup lighting kicked in - pulsing an eerie red glow throughout the station in intervals of a few seconds. Hooper wiped some of the commander's blood off her face, took a deep breath and pressed on, floating silently through the various modules until she reached the sound of the destruction. The pulsing red lights and tight corridors gave everything a more sinister feel.

Upon entering the room, Hooper gasped. There were parts of machinery, computers, and plastic floating in the air. She quickly scanned the room from left to right, expecting to see her frenzied friend causing more chaos, but he was nowhere to be seen. Maybe he bled out?

Then, from above, Jones lunged at Hooper with another sickening cry. His hands fixed into claws as if he were an eagle diving towards a timid mouse, but Hooper wasn't having any of it. She quickly flashed the screwdriver upwards, catching Jones across the cheek. Blood squirted out his face like a long red, shiny streamer, causing Jones to roar with pain.

"Arggh! You'll pay for that, you bitch!"

"Jones! Stop! This is madness. Why are you doing this? Geez, is that even you in there?"

As soon as Hooper asked, she already knew the answer. It wasn't him. How could it be? But she had to ask. No. The thing out there had claimed her crew mate.

"Raagghhh!" Jones arched backwards as he screamed. Then he glimpsed the thing outside through the window. Like a light switch being flicked off, it caused him to stop mid-roar and stare longingly at his master.

This was Hooper's chance. She would not wait for him to attack again. Quickly, she needed to free him and end this. She pressed off the wall with both feet and flew forward, screwdriver first, towards Jones' exposed neck. With a sickening squelch, she hit the target, embedding the screwdriver deep into his throat and with the momentum of the push still pressing her forward she catapulted around Jones, whilst still holding the screwdriver, gouging a seven-inch gash around his neck. She grasped the wall, knowing the deed was done, and could only give her thrashing, screaming crew member a quick glance before bursting into tears. Jones eventually stopped convulsing and floated motionlessly.

After a few minutes, Hooper, now covered with a mixture

of Jones' and Mackenzie's blood and her own tears, composed herself and scowled out a window.

"So… just me and you now then, huh?" Hooper said, as she looked at the thing. "Well, fuck you!"

She pushed off and floated out of the module. Unable to remain there any longer, she returned to the comms room. She picked up the radio, more out of habit than anything else, and began her final log.

"Houston… Luna Habitat crew… *Anyone*… This is Nicole Hooper of the International Space Station. Jones, Vasili and Commander Mackenzie are all dead and I'm all that's left of the crew… Well, screw it, I'm all that's left of the species…" Hooper paused for a moment to catch her breath and remain professional. "To whoever is listening, we encountered an alien life-form which has destroyed our home planet. It is roughly squid-like in appearance, with long seeking tendrils, but myself and my crew have been unable to truly fathom its incomprehensible form. In fact, I believe trying to do so was what caused my crew mate Jones to lose his mind. It is still present in our space and I expect this station will be its next target."

Hooper pulled the radio away from her mouth and looked out the window. The being turned his vast head towards the station…

"…OK. It appears I was right. It has turned and is gliding towards me now. Oh god, this is it."

Hooper felt urine leaking into her trousers.

"…This is Hooper of the ISS. Of Earth. And this is our FIRST and LAST contact."

This was the end…

…this was the final log.

Hunted

Three rounds left.

"Shit, I thought I had it!" Ethan cursed, as he primed the bolt on his rifle, watching bark explode in the distance from the impact of that precious bullet.

In truth, he was no-where near hitting the mark - just another rustle in the bushes. When the wind picked up, the forest would sway and dance in the breeze, almost as if it were breathing. Under normal circumstances, it would feel serene, which is why Ethan enjoyed going out on hunting trips whenever he could leave the house. Lately, it felt more like home than *home*.

The sun shone through the mottled leaves above, casting a speckled effect down onto the forest floor, and Ethan could see that the small dirt path he had been tracking the beast down had long vanished. This was very much off-piste. This was the wilderness.

Ethan noticed his gun was shaking.

Adrenaline?

Anxiety?

Fear?

Crouching low, he wiped his brow and took a deep breath - filling his lungs with the pine scented fresh air. That thing took Carrie and what father would he be if he just gave up the chase?

"That fucker is going to pay! Thinks it can come into my forest and steal my girl? Not gonna happen!" Ethan stood up, steadied his rifle, and pressed on through the trees. "Not on my watch!"

Up ahead, he could hear the thing howl an ungodly howl. Ethan had hunted these woods for over ten years, but never had he heard an animal noise like that before. It didn't matter; Nothing would stop him from hunting this beast and saving his daughter.

He picked up the pace.

He could hear it up ahead.

It must have only been fifty feet away...

Forty feet...

Thirty...

SNAP

The crunch of the wood splitting under Ethan's boot sounded like another gunshot.

"Fuck!"

Ethan instinctively raised his rifle and fired in the vague direction of the roar.

Two rounds left.

There was no misplaced hope with this shot. He knew he completely *whiffed* it.

The thing stopped roaring, and Ethan could hear it bounding off again. Dammit! Carrie was so close!

"Geez, what the fuck am I doing? Think, you dumb fuck," Ethan said, smacking his own head over and over. "You're gonna hit your girl if you keep this up!"

How could he have been so careless? Had he become so much

like his father?

Shoot first, ask questions later.

Why had he even brought his daughter on this trip? A hunt was no place for a nine-year-old, but he really craved some father-daughter time and things were so fractious at home he just had to get away. She looked so cute in her new hunting gear, though - so proud to spend some time with daddy.

Ethan pulled out his cell phone. "Shit, still no signal". He stared longingly at his lock screen - an image of him with Carrie riding on his shoulders. She looked so happy.

Ethan put the phone back in his jacket pocket and rested his hand on a giant pine tree to steady his nerves when his fingertips felt something.

There were markings on the tree bark.

Carvings.

Sigils.

Runes?

"Who the hell bothers to carve stuff all the way out here?" Ethan pondered, tracing the carving with his fingers. "Damn kids!"

He pulled his hand away, and it felt *sticky*. The sap from this tree looked just like... blood. It was blood! Ethan initially thought he'd hit Carrie, but a closer look at the tree showed the blood fused into the carving, staining the bark, like some sort of ancient offering. It was fresh, too...

"Ugh, fucking pagan freaks!"

Ethan had read reports in one of his local hunting magazines about some religious nut jobs operating deep in the forest some-where and just guessed that this was their insane handiwork. The report mentioned secret meetings, missing people and strange devil worshiping that had been going since the 70's. All nonsense as far as Ethan was concerned - just another load of clickbait to give people something else to be fearful of.

"If I ever bump into one of these weirdos, I'll introduce them to the butt of my gun!" Ethan growled, as he wiped the blood on his Deerhunter camo trousers. "Ugh, this is disgusting…"

Ethan steadied his nerve, lifted the rifle up, and peered through the scope. The path forward was clear. The thing had ripped through the bushes up ahead, so tracking it would be easy. Ethan pressed on.

The dense vegetation all around him was nearly impassable. All except the pathway the thing had created. One thing was obvious - it must have been big. *Really* big. But for all the time he had been hunting it, he hadn't actually got eyes on the thing yet.

Around him, nearly every tree now had runes carved up the entire trunk. Almost every inch of bark contained some scrawl, or scratching of some sort, saying something in a language Ethan, or every few other humans, could interpret. The sticky red blood was oozing down onto the forest floor, pooling at the bases of the trees and over their gnarled roots. It almost sparkled in the mottled sunlight.

"Daddy! Daddy!"

It sounded like Carrie!

Hearing her cry both filled Ethan with rage and fear in equal measure, but his protective father's instincts took over.

He sprinted towards the sound of his kidnapped daughter - the one thing he loved more than hunting, more than anything on this earth.

She was still alive!

Bursting through the last hedge, Ethan stumbled on a root but caught his fall just in time. As he lifted his head, he saw a cave, nearly fifteen feet high, and standing in the mouth of it was... *the thing.*

Towering ten feet tall and swathed in matted fur the color of dead pine bark, the ancient creature stood hunched on its hind legs before the gaping maw of a cave, its breath steaming in the cold forest air. Its eyes were small, sunken, and glinting like wet coal - never blinking, staring right at Ethan. Clawed hands, far too long for a natural beast, twitched at its sides, and its mouth, jagged and wide, stretched in a grotesque approximation of a grin. It wasn't just a monster; it was the thing the wilderness had been hiding. The thing the sigils on the trees were made for...

It opened its mouth and spoke in a rough imitation of a human tongue, "Daddy! Daddy!"

Ethan stared, dumbfounded. "What. The. Fuck..."

If he was waiting for the perfect shot, this would have been it, but Ethan couldn't...

The thing laughed, causing Ethan to stumble sideways and slip on a pool of tree blood.

One round left.

Ethan looked down. His poor trigger control caused his hand to convulse at the slip and fire a shot into the floor.

The shot sent the thing bounding into the cave.

Into its home.

"You fucker, get back here. Give me back my daughter!" he yelled into the darkness of the cave entrance as he primed the final round into the chamber. "I know you're in there!"

Ethan lifted the rifle and fired into the darkness. Then listened...

No rounds left.

"Daddy!" the thing said, in that horribly garbled mockery of her daughter.

"Fuck." Ethan knew the thing was still there. "I'm coming in and then you'll be sorry!"

With tears running down his cheeks, he sprinted into the cave and instantly stumbled over something near the entrance. As he fell, his hand went straight into something warm, wet and sticky - a steaming carcass of an indistinct animal... or human.

He looked around for his daughter, but could only see dirt, bones, and blood covering the floor. It was only at this moment, lit by the fading, mottled sunlight from the trees behind him, that he realized the truth. Looking around at the blood and the entrails whilst tasting the fetid smell of death in the air, Ethan knew he had fallen right into the feeding pit.

Clack clack clack - the sound of the things' claws chittering with excitement that another meal had presented itself, as it stepped forwards towards Ethan. The wet eyes glinting in the darkness.

"Daaaaaadddyyy," the thing laughed. *Clack clack clack*

Ethan scowled at the thing emerging from the darkness. "I have you now, you dumb fuck..." and in one swift motion primed the rifle and raised it towards the thing's jet-black eyes.

Click

Ethan gasped and instinctively primed the rifle again and fired.

Click

"Oh, shit..." Ethan's eyes bulged wide as he knew that this was it.

Carrie was gone, and he would be next.

He had been hunted.

The Sleeper's Breath

"Captain, we are nearing the trench," informed Sarin, not looking up from his monitor. "Descending at our current speed, we should reach the probe in an hour."

Western Pacific Ocean...
Eleven thousand meters down...
Sixteen thousand PSI...
A new frontier...
...Four crew members in a tin can at the bottom of the
world.

"Thank you, Doctor." Captain Elena Voss stood at the front of the bridge, on the sub-aquatic research vessel 'Deepspire', her gaze fixed on the blinking controls before her. She was used to pressure, both the literal and the psychological, but even the seasoned leader couldn't ignore the oppressive weight of what lay underneath them - a previously unexplored crack at the bottom of the earth dubbed 'The Abyssal Trench'.

"Last check, people," Voss said, her voice sharp, steady. "We're at the bottom of the Mariana now, nearing the entrance to the new trench. You all know what to expect... Heavy pressure, poor visibility, and the usual technical glitches. Stay sharp and keep the chatter to a minimum. Remember, we're not here to explore ancient mysteries. We're here to recover the lost probe and get some answers for the boffins above. They need to learn about these new seismic shifts, and quickly."

Dr. Malik Sarin, seated at the back of the bridge, didn't look up from his monitor. His fingers traced the map of sonar readings from their descent, his brow furrowed. "Voss, these readings though…" He paused, his voice low, barely above a whisper. "They don't match anything we've seen. Look, I know you all like to poke fun at my love of ancient civilizations, but even the data from the probe down there seems completely off. It's not just the geology… these readings show there's something alive down there. The pulse is rhythmic. L-like… Like breathing."

"Noted," Voss replied, her gaze flicking to the sonar monitor as the pulse echoed faintly through the hull. "But we're not hunting ghosts, Sarin. Nothing can be alive down at this depth… I'm not interested in fairytales."

"If nothing is going to be alive in the trench, why is *she* here?" Sarin muttered under his breath, pushing his small, circular spectacles up the bridge of his nose and glancing over at the rather meek figure on the other side of the bridge.

Ava Reyes, a marine biologist, didn't respond right away. She was staring at the life-support console, her fingers frozen over the keys. Her face was pale, eyes wide, as if she was hearing something more than just the hum of the submarine's systems. "I don't know…" she whispered, almost to herself. "There's something off about this place. I keep feeling like… something is *watching* us. Down in the deep."

Laird, the engineer, drafted into the team from Scotland,

shifted uneasily on his seat, tapping his fingers against the cold metal of his console. "I hate to admit it, but I've got to agree with Reyes. These readings are all wrong. Pressure's rising, but not uniformly. The hull's creaking at random intervals. The sub doesn't feel right, Captain."

Voss turned sharply, her gaze hard. "Focus, people! We've been over this. We have a job to do, and that job doesn't include getting spooked by every groan the hull makes. I know this is all a massive unknown for us all. No other humans have even seen this new trench, let alone go into it, but it's imperative we retrieve that probe. We can't have any more cracks opening." She stared out the window at the floor of the Mariana Trench below and sighed. "OK. Laird, check the seals again. Reyes, monitor everyone's stats, tell me if anyone spikes. Sarin, keep your eyes on that terrain. If there's another seismic shift, I want to know about it. I don't want any surprises, people. We don't have time for paranoia."

There was a long, uneasy silence as the Deepspire cut through the pressure of the ocean like a knife. The four crew members busied themselves with their individual tasks whilst outside, the shadows of the trench stretched infinitely in all directions - a vast, impenetrable void. Each crew member had thousands of hours of deep-water experience, but there was something about this dive, the unknown element perhaps, that caused tensions to feel far higher. The recirculated air felt thick and oppressive, and the walls of the sub seemed to shrink inwards. They didn't know what they were heading towards, down in the dark, but inside; the ship groaned in response to the pressure - more than just metal buckling at that depth. It sounded... like a breath.

Voss cleared her throat. "Here we go, team. Into the

unknown!"

Reyes couldn't help but let out a little chuckle at that unintentional movie quote. She actually thought Elena Voss would have made a good Elsa - she certainly had the ice-cold coolness under pressure, and she definitely gave the impression of someone who needs to 'let it go' once in a while.

With an eerie silence, the Deepspire began its descent through the newly formed crack, towards the unexplored cavernous area beneath the known world.

"Just think, we're deeper than any human has ever dreamed of," said Sarin, marveled at the prestige and renown a trip like this can offer. "Let's just hope the ship's integrity holds…"

"Well, she hasn't fallen apart yet!" Joked Laird. "This sub must obviously have one hell of an engineer!"

"Quiet people," commanded Voss, as she skillfully navigated the ship through the crevice. Once clear of the jagged rocks, she continued, "Laird, could you d-…"

"Yes?" Interrupted Reyes.

The other three looked at her, confused.

"Sorry, did you say something?" Reyes clarified. Their puzzled faces staring back at her had her confused now, too.

The crew looked at one another, with only the slight hum of the engines breaking the awkward silence.

"…*Well*, there we have it. Ava was the first to crack!" Laird laughed. "I knew I should have offered bets."

Voss glared menacingly at Laird, causing him to shrink a little and stifle the laughter to a minor giggle. She turned at Reyes and said, "No one said anything, Ava. It's OK."

"Oh… I see," Reyes blushed. "I could have sworn… Sorry, must have been dreaming." She let out a little nervous chuckle to cover up her embarrassment.

Voss was about to continue her command for Laird to double-check the interior pressure, but Sarin was the first to speak.

"There is something truly unique about the geology down here. Look, captain."

Captain Voss spun her chair towards Sarin's workstation, at the back of the bridge, and examined the monitor.

She squinted at the screen. "Help me out, Doctor. What am I looking at here?"

Sarin tapped the monitor. "These aren't normal rock formations, captain… Take a closer look. If I had to label them, the shape of them, I mean, I'd say they look like… a structure…"

"Piss off, Doc," roared Laird, in his thick Scottish accent from the other side of the bridge. "There's no bloody way there's a man-made structure down here. Humans didn't even know this place existed, let alone could navigate to this depth."

"…I didn't say 'man' made it," Sarin said. His words hanging in the air for a moment.

"Right. OK. So, the great Dr Malik Sarin and this crazy love for ancient civilizations were the second to crack. You know, you guys ar-…"

"LAIRD!" shouted Voss. "This is your final warning. Keep it professional or so help me God, I'll lock you away somewhere. We don't have a brig, but I'm sure I could find a cupboard or something!"

"Sarin," Voss said, as she let out a sigh and composed herself. "Is it possible that it's just a freak coincidence and that the geology down here just *looks* like a building?"

"I suppose it's possible, but…"

Just then, the proximity warnings beeped into life as a large, dark shape darted across the cockpit window. It was only there a moment, but it was easily fifty feet long and moving at an incredible speed.

"Holy crap! What the hell was that?" cried Laird. "A creature? Reyes was that a creature down here?! That's impossible, right?"

Ava Reyes swallowed. She was hoping that she could go on this entire trip by just sitting quietly and not being called upon. She loved nature, but that love didn't really extend to people outside the animal kingdom. It's why her friends always claimed she wasn't exactly a 'people person'. "Er, it was only on the monitor for a second. I... I don't really know," she said, too nervous to glance up from the monitor in case she missed it a second time.

Sensing that Laird would react poorly to that vulnerable statement, Voss immediately stepped in. "Reyes, ignore him. Could you do a full scan of this area, please? Perhaps we're looking at a new species!"

Reyes smiled at the thought of finding a new species, and her mood lightened slightly. "Yes, captain."

The first invisible wave flowed over the Deepspire, from somewhere down in the deeps.

"What should I do about the leak, though?" Reyes continued.

Laird sat bolt upright in his seat. "Leak? What *leak?*" His engineering hackles fully up.

Reyes looked at Laird with a puzzled face. "Erm... The one the captain was just talking about. She said there was something leaking on the floor... and that it came from the kitchen."

Laird leaped from his seat and sprinted to the back of the ship towards the food prep area.

Sarin walked over to Reyes and put his hand on her shoulder. "Darling, there was no talk of a leak..."

Reyes winced at the touch and even more so at being called

'Darling'. It reminded her of her old, stuffy biology teacher at university, who was also quite handsy. She said nothing though, like always, and just lowered her head and began the scan of the new area. Two embarrassments in two minutes… it was times like this she wished the ocean could just swallow her whole.

After a few moments, there were some choice expletives being yelled from the back of the sub as Laird finished his investigation into the phantom leak. Of course, the crew had no idea what Laird was actually shouting, because of the thick accent, but they knew he wasn't best pleased. Laird hated having to move when it wasn't absolutely necessary.

Upon walking back to his station, Sarin gasped at the monitor. "Captain, these readings show that there is definitely a structure down here. A massive structure. And what's more, the probe is smack bang in the middle of it!"

"OK, I'm taking us down for a closer look," Voss said with a commanding voice, tilting the throttle forward a little to increase the descent speed. "Whatever it is, I want us all on our guard. Let's get in, grab the probe data, and get out."

As The Deepspire sank further into the eternal black, the beams of its floodlights finally found something solid… something impossible. The abyssal gloom gave way to shapes, first jagged and indistinct, like the fractured teeth of some buried colossus. But as the lights steadied, the crew beheld an ancient city.

"By the heavens… look at this place," Sarin said as he stood, staring at this new world. His mouth opened in awe. "I was right. I *knew* I was right!"

The structures loomed like titanic tombstones carved by a forgotten god. Geometry broken and wrong, angles that hurt to look at and seemed to shift when not directly observed. Nothing obeyed symmetry or scale. Pillars thicker than redwoods spiraled skyward, only to bend back down into themselves. Monoliths jutted out of the seabed at impossible inclinations, their surfaces etched with glyphs that shimmered with a sickly phosphorescence and glyphs that twisted into patterns the human brain instinctively rejected.

Age had not eroded the buildings in any natural way, but seemed to have melted or folded the walls, as if science worked differently here. Archways opened into pitch-black voids, larger on the inside than the outside. Vast stairways led nowhere, vanishing into rock or reappearing dozens of meters away, mocking the logic of space.

"W-w…What Is this place?" questioned Reyes. Her voice quivered as she stumbled over the words.

Through the cockpit glass, it felt as though the city wasn't resting on the seafloor, but growing from it, almost like a fungal infestation of alien architecture. Something about the scale made the crew feel miniature, irrelevant. These weren't ruins built for humans, or even for any known lifeform. They were the petrified dreams of an entity far older than time, petrified mid-thought.

Another wave, invisible to the naked eye, washed over the ship.

To the crew, it felt like a slow, rhythmic vibration humming through the sub's frame. The structures weren't just old… they were waiting to be found.

"I've been drowning in stars," Laird whispered as he stumbled in from the rear of the sub. "A beautiful dream. A beautiful dream."

The rest of the crew turned to witness the horror that was

Laird's face. His entire left cheek was hanging off, blood pouring onto the steel floor, making a sound like a tap running in a metallic sink, leaving a thick oozy trail behind him. Random patterns of bloodied claw marks covered the rest of Laird's skin.

"Jesus Christ! Reyes, get the bandages from the medkit. Sarin, check in the back, see what's back there," Voss commanded. "Make sure we don't have a stowaway on-board."

"Captain," Sarin calmly said. "Look at his hands. I think this is self-inflicted."

Reyes rushed over and tried to stem the bleeding from Laird's face but couldn't help noticing his fingertips, which still had chunks of flesh and hair under the nails.

"Sarin's right, Captain. It looks like he's torn half his face off with his bare hands." Reyes agreed. Then, out of nowhere, her eyes rolled back into her skull.

A wave from below washed over the sub.

"The walls breathe when I'm not looking," Reyes chanted. "I saw the metal pulse like lungs. The ocean will swallow me whole."

"Reyes, what the hell? Snap out of it and stop that bloody leak in his face!" Voss said. Her ragged, tense breathing displayed her utter confusion about what was happening to her crew. "It's leaking all over the floor. And Sarin, just check in the back, dammit. That's an order. I'm going to radio up to the surface."

Sarin calmly moved to the rear of the sub, trying hard to not slip on the bloodied mess Laird left behind as Voss turned to grab the radio and send a distress message up to the surface.

"US Willow, this is Captain Voss of The Deepspire research vessel. We've passed through the crevice into a previously unexplored area of the seabed but have an emergency on board. Owen Laird has become injured and looks in a critical situation… requesting advice."

"Gzzzkkk… dreee… gzzzkkk am…. with Re… gzzzkkk" replied the garbled message, broken by bursts of static.

"I'm sorry, US Willow, could you repeat?"

"Gzzzkkk… R-Rey… gzzzkkk… Reyes… Gzzzkkk."

"…*Reyes?*" Voss replied, horrified at hearing the distinct name of one of her crew in the static, garbled mess.

Breaking the confused exchange on the radio, Sarin came running back onto the bridge.

"Laird! Let go of her!"

Voss turned to witness Laird's hands clamped on either side of Ava Reyes' face, as he stood nose to nose, eyes locked, as he whispered words the crew couldn't understand. Reyes' eyes were wide with fear as a puddle of urine started leaking onto the floor, mixing with the blood. Whatever he was saying to her, she couldn't look away.

Before Voss could do anything, the radio behind her responded.

"Gzzzkkkk… Reyes will be the first to dream."

Another wave pulsed across the ship.

With a sickening crack, Laird twisted and snapped Reyes' neck before tossing her to one side like a rag doll.

"NO!" Sarin and Voss both yelled in unison. Before Sarin tackled the grinning Laird to the floor.

The pair crashed onto the steel flooring, sliding in the bloody mess from Laird's face.

"The stars are down here now. They blink beneath the waves," Laird was almost chanting, his head thrashing side to side as he spoke, blood spraying with every turn. "We never left the surface. This is a dream. A dream inside his dream."

"He…*murdered* her." Voss said, staring dumbfounded. "Ava… Poor Ava"

"My God, he's totally lost it," Sarin yelled. "What should we do, Captain? Captain!"

"Ph'nglui mglw'nafh… yes, yes," Laird continued, growing louder. "Ia… Ia… his name tastes like salt and rust. Say it with me. SAY IT WITH ME!"

Voss snapped out of it and darted over and helped Sarin secure Laird onto the floor. "Those words, Sarin. What on earth was that? He's speaking absolute gibberish."

Sarin recoiled and rose to his feet, leaving Voss with Laird. "I… I *know* those words." He started walking backwards, eyes wide with a mix of excitement and fear. He turned and darted over to his desk and fumbled around for a tatty old notebook, flipped a few pages in and thrust the book at Voss "Look!"

"I'm… kinda… busy," Voss said, straining to hold the engineer down. "What is it?!"

"It's not gibberish… just forgotten words," Sarin explained as he adjusted his spectacles and read. "Translated, Captain, it means - 'In his house-'" Sarin read.

A wave washed over the sub, the pattern becoming more rhythmic the deeper they sank.

"…CTHULHU OF R'LYEH WAITS DREAMING," interrupted Laird, as he roared with delight. "We have to open the hatch and wake him."

"Sarin… who or what the fuck is Cthulhu?" Voss snapped at the doctor. "Explain to me this instant! And make goddamn sure that Laird goes nowhere near that hatch, OK?"

For the first time in her career, Captain Elena Voss had no grasp on the situation and no idea what to do next. She felt lost and alone. How could she salvage this mission?

"Captain, what we saw on the monitor. The pulses. It wasn't sonar. I think it was a heartbeat. *His* heartbeat," Sarin explained. "That structure out there... I think. I think..."

"I knowww, I knowwww," laughed Laird, his arms thrashing up to paw at Voss' face, leaving smears of blood with every touch.

"... is the ancient city of R'lyeh."

"Sarin, I have no fucking idea what that is. Can you stop with all this mythological bullshit and come and hold Laird?" Voss said, her voice almost rising to a panicked shout.

"... b-but it can't be R'lyeh," Sarin pondered as he flicked through his journal. "It shouldn't be here, look. Miskatonic University claims it should be near the Pacific pole of inaccessibility - That's over ten thousand kilometers away."

"Get over here and keep him down! I need to get us out of here and up to the surface."

"What? No! You can't, captain." Sarin said, visibly shocked at the suggestion. "We can't go!"

"Are you mad?!" Voss' shock was clear. "We have to abort the mission. We've lost one crew member already. I can't lose any more."

"Captain, this is the find of a lifetime. Of a species! We can't abandon it. We must inform Miskatonic that they were wrong... We can't leave the dream behind." Sarin said.

Another wave washed over the sub from below.

"There's no such thing as 'up' anymore. Only down. Only deeper." Sung Laird.

"Captain, I think we were destined to find him. It was always going to be us. It's why we were born. Can't you see?" Sarin's voice was growing more and more fanatical. "He's calling... we need to wake him up."

Voss stood, leaving the thrashing Laird on the floor and walked dejected over to the cockpit. She stared into her reflection... and it blinked first as another wave, a breath, washed over the sub.

"What is going on?" Voss said, her mind breaking with every wave that washed over the sub. "I want to go up to the surface."

"... but you can't can you, captain." Sarin mused. "The control stick is just there, but you won't use it. He won't let you."

"There's too much water inside me. I'm sinking from the inside out. Ia... Ia...." Laird screeched, rolling across the floor.

A long wave, almost like a breath, enveloped the sub.

"Sarin... is this why you volunteered?" Voss said, without turning around. "Did you know?"

Sarin grabbed the pen from his notebook and started scrawling on the steel hull. "It's a map. The real one. Made of screams. Dreams and screams in the deep."

"There was no probe, was there, Sarin? Did we dream it?" Voss wondered.

Everything seemed so hopeless. One crew member was dead, the other two succumbed to madness, and Voss was quickly losing her own grip on reality. She almost discovered enough will to grab the control stick when the lights of the sub showed her worst fears...

"I... I *see* him," Voss said, barely louder than a whisper. "He's here."

Through the thick, pressure-scarred glass of the cockpit window, the abyss parted like a curtain as the floodlights carved through only a fraction of the darkness... but it was enough.

There he was.

Cthulhu didn't loom. He occupied. Space and sense distorted around him. At first, he seemed like a crumbled mountain of flesh, sprawled across a cyclopean city of impossible angles and obscene architecture. Then his form shifted, no, unfolded, as if what Voss was looking at was merely a project, a fraction, a dream-stain leaking into their reality.

His wings, vast and membranous, curled around him like a shroud. His limbs were not at rest but poised in stillness, each clawed finger twitching with some slow rhythm - like a hand clenching in sleep. His head, a mass of tentacles, undulated gently, as though swaying in a current that wasn't there.

He was sleeping. And dreaming. And breathing - each breath sending out waves into the ocean above, distorting time and space.

An immense wave, expelled from Cthulhu, crashed into The Deepspire.

Voss didn't hear it with her ears, but she felt it in her bones. The pulse, similar to before but much stronger this time - older than time, reverberating throughout the metal hull, through her marrow, through thought itself. Alien vision scraped against her mind's eye: stars bleeding, planets weeping oceans into the void, and endless, green-lit corridors spiraling into madness.

"His eyes are closed!" Voss exclaimed. "Thank God, his eyes are closed!"

"And yet, he sees us. Doesn't he, captain?" Sarin said, moving up alongside her, placing a bloodied hand on her shoulder.

"Ph'nglui mglw'nafh Cthulhu R'lyeh wgah'nagl fhtagn," Laird croaked, before bleeding out where Voss left him - finally succumbing to death.

Cthulhu sighed, causing another dreamlike wave into the sub.

"Two dead... I feel so small," Voss said, tears forming in her eyes.

"…We're not small. We're nothing," Sarin replied.

The ocean around the sub was utterly still.

The dreaming God waited.

And the sub kept sinking…

"We are inside the dream… and it's breathing through us."

Silence.

Then… the sound of one long, impossible breath and the opening of a single eye.

Whispers Beneath The Mountain

The *smell* hit first.

Iron. Shit. Burning hair.

Then came the screaming.

"Goblins!" Silas muttered, already notching an arrow before the others in the party had even drawn breath. His Elven ears picking out the distinct sound of green-skins on the road ahead. The screams, however, were very much human.

The party of four rounded the bend, towards the noise, and stumbled into… *chaos*. An overturned cart blazed in the mud, one wheel spinning lazily in the firelight. Beside it, a gutted horse twitched feebly, trying to rise before collapsing with a wet, broken moan in the dirt. Alongside the dying horse, a woman lay face-down in a widening pool of blood with an axe buried deep between her shoulder blades. Amid the carnage stood a single survivor - a middle-aged man, weeping, swinging a chipped sword. He fought not with hope, but defiance - slashing at the air with a panicked look in his eyes. The Goblins mocked him, jeering and shrieking. Six, maybe seven. It was hard to count through the fiery haze from the car.

"Enough," Draxian growled as he cracked his neck and charged at the pack.

The first goblin never saw the axe. It hit low, fueled by pure

Dwarven fury, shearing leg from hip in a spray of black-red gore. The goblin squealed with agony as it collapsed onto the floor, alerting the others.

The second barely had time to blink before Silas' arrow burst through its skull, popping its head like a rotten fruit.

"For The Lightmother!" Elysia cried, rushing into the fray. Her mace crashed down onto a Goblin's head with righteous force, bone crunching and splintering beneath the blow. Holy fire seared the wound, turning flesh to ash as the creature fell in a smoldering heap at her feet, like a rag-doll.

Kelebor hesitated at the rear, his hands trembling. "I…I…I c-can't…"

Magic had a price, and he'd already paid it once. He knew he needed to control his power… but when three Goblins peeled away and charged the robed mage; there was no choice. Out of instinct, more than anything else, he whispered an incantation, raised his hands, and closed his eyes as blisteringly hot arcane fire erupted from his fingers, engulfing the goblins mid-laugh. Instant incineration twisted their glee into shrieks as their skin melted from bone.

Kelebor staggered, breath ragged. Another strand of hair turned silver.

That's *two* now. He swallowed hard.

"Be more careful," he thought.

And then…

Silence.

The six goblins were gone in a matter of seconds. The survivor looked around at the carnage, dropped his sword down in the mud, and began sobbing uncontrollably.

Elysia moved forward and kneeled beside the dead woman, her gauntlet brushing blood-matted hair from her face as she murmured a prayer.

The traumatized man picked himself up, walked over to Elysia, and clutched at her cloak as he said, "That's my wife… She was so brave… I-I couldn't save her, though."

The half-elf cleric looked up at the man and said, "You *both* were incredibly brave. Your wife is at peace now."

"Will she… will she hear that? Your prayer, I mean?"

Elysia looked toward the horizon. Beyond the distant trees - Valkyr's Rise, its jagged mountainous peak clawing at storm-torn clouds.

"She hears," Elysia said, softly. "But sometimes… even the Gods ask for help."

Silas scoffed behind her. "And we're supposed to be the help?" He wiped his Elven dagger on a goblin's tunic. "Your vision told you what's supposed to be up there. If true, what could the four of us do against that?"

"…*Try*," she said, simply.

"Against an imprisoned God?" Silas huffed.

Kelebor, still at the rear of the carnage, said nothing. His gaze locked on the smoldering goblin corpses he created. His hands trembling.

Bodies…

Just like before…

"I think it suits you," roared Draxian, walking up and playfully punching his arm. "The hair, I mean. Silver is a good look."

"Oh. Thanks…" Kelebor raised his hand up to his hair, welcoming the distraction from his thoughts. "I can feel it inside me, too. The extra power. It's hard to describe but I know it's there."

"Well, don't burn through all your magic just yet," Draxian said, as he slung his axe over his shoulder and glanced over to Silas and Elysia. "It looks like brother and sister over there are taking us all the way up the mountain. We'll definitely be needing more of your Ashblood magic shit!"

"Silvermanes," Kelebor muttered to himself, whilst rubbing his punched arm. "We prefer 'Silvermanes'..." As he spoke, Kelebor's mind flashed to the memory of The Silvered Guild. His apprenticeship. The... *accident.*

Draxian turned and began walking back to the others.

"Hey, Drax," Kelebor called out. "I'm curious. Why did you sign up for this quest? I thought you dwarves didn't believe in gods and the like?"

"We don't. But we sure love a quest!" Draxian said, turning to face the mage again. "Think of the glory! I reckon if we pull it off, they'll be singing about our adventure for years to come. Elysia needed an axe, so here I am. Anyway, how about you? Why is a scrawny ashblood apprentice volunteering to come out here? When me and the other two arrived at the Guild, you couldn't wait to put yourself forward for our quest. We reckoned we were going to struggle to find one of you lot to join us, but you leaped at the chance. You just wanted to burn up a bunch of goblins, huh?" A smirk flashed across Draxian's face.

"I...er..." Kelebor stammered, looking down at the three charred corpses.

"Ha, I'm just kidding with you, laddie." Draxian roared. "I know how you mage folk have your own weird reasons for stuff. Don't need to be so sensitive."

Exile. Atonement. That's the real reason I'm here... I murdered them and they would have imprisoned me if I had stayed.

"Tell me," Kelebor asked, nodding towards their other two companions. "What do you know of Silas and Elysia?"

Draxian glanced backwards, making sure they were out of earshot. "Mr and Miss Emberbrook?" Draxian wiped the ale dripping from his beard. "Step-siblings. Elysia is a half-elf, whilst Silas is a full elf."

"…and he has excellent hearing," interrupted Silas, in the distance. "Tell me, I've always wondered, can dwarves whisper? Like, is it actually possible to be discrete? Or do you *have* to shout everything?"

"…Hmph. I enjoy shouting. Let's my enemies know I'm about to cut them in two," Draxian said, straightening up a little.

Kelebor grinned. "What about her vision?"

Draxian shrugged. "No idea, lad. Better ask her."

Up ahead, Elysia rose to her feet and lifted the distraught villager to his. "You are injured," Elysia said, looking down at a slash across the man's belly.

"Oh… yeah," the man replied. "Weird, I didn't even notice it."

"That can happen, but it's OK." Elysia lifted her hands to the wound. "Let me…"

The man lifted his shirt and a warm, soft glow flowed from Elysia's hands into the wound, sealing it shut.

"Wow. I've never been healed by magic before," the man said, inspecting his stomach.

"Oh. This isn't magic," Elysia replied, lowering her head so the man could see her golden hair. "No silver here, see. I'm a cleric - Our power comes from my God, The Lightmother. I am simply the vessel for her to channel her powers through."

"C-C-Can you do anything for my wife?" The man said expectantly, looking down at her bloodied corpse again. "…I can pay."

Elysia laid a hand on the man's shoulder. "I'm sorry. Even The Lightmother can't reverse death."

"Oh…" the small flicker of hope behind the man's eyes faded as quick as it appeared.

"What will do you do now?" Elysia asked.

"I guess I'll take her back to her father. He'll want to bury her properly," the man said, wiping tears from his eyes. "She deserves better than rotting in the mud next to some filthy green-skins."

"Yes, indeed. You are a good man, my friend," she said, her face glowing with a warm and friendly smile. "Tell me though, before you go, where were you coming from? Goblins shouldn't be this far south."

"Brimholt."

"Brimholt? You mean The Weeping Vale?" Inquired Elysia. "Why were you traveling from there? I heard a curse lingers there…"

"This place *is* cursed, my lady," the man replied, his eyes widening. "It deserves the nickname of The Weeping Vale, I can assure you. There's something wrong with the mountain. There have been rumors of a darkness festering at the summit."

I know. She told me.

"I see." Elysia glanced up to the mountain.

"Please, if you're heading that way, can you investigate the curse? I used to know a lot of good people in Brimhol… I mean The Weeping Vale."

Elysia turned to look at the man and smiled. "That's why we're here."

For a moment, the man smiled back.

Hope.

"Now I suggest you take your dear wife and make for the village of Dunlowe, before more Goblins come," Elysia said, pointing to the path behind her. "It's half a day's travel back that way. The people there will take care of you."

"Yes, my lady." the man nodded.

"Then farewell, friend. My The Lightmother watch over you."

The man carefully, and with reference, removed the axe, picked up his wife, placed her over his shoulder and walked down the path towards the nearby village.

"You were wise to not tell him about the vision, El," Silas said, walking up alongside his sister. "The more people we tell, the more likely we'll end up telling the *wrong* people."

"I know… It's my burden. *Our* burden. Let's leave the common folk out of it."

"…I still think it's a mistake," Silas said, straightening up. "We should leave this land alone. What if it is a problem that cannot be solved?"

"My God showed…"

"Your God showed you nothing, El," Silas snapped, cutting off Elysia mid-sentence. "It was a dream!"

"Silas…" Elysia smiled warmly at her brother. "If you saw it too, you would have known the truth, but you've never believed."

"No, I believe in nature. In things I can touch. In animals, I can see and hear. You have your religion, and I have mine…" Silas said, holding out his arms to the surrounding landscape.

"Tell me, dear brother, why *does* this journey terrify you so?" Elysia said.

"…because… because I can't protect you against what's up there, El! Goblins, undead, beasts are simple, but what good is an arrow against a God?"

"Who says we'll need arrows?" Elysia said with a sly smile.

Silas rolled his eyes. "Oh, El. I know there's no convincing you. We need to be prepared though, OK? Promise me that. It could be anything up there, right?" Silas asked. "Maybe it isn't a god at all."

"No, it is… The Lightmother is worried, Silas and I believe her. I have faith in what she's showing me. Enough for both of us."

"Fine! Look, I don't know if this quest is wise, but whatever happens, I'll always be by your side."

"Thank you, brother," Elysia said. "Someone has imprisoned a God and no-one knows why. We need to unravel this mystery."

Kelebor approached from behind and softly spoke, "I think the bigger question we need to ask is, *how* can someone or something imprison a God?"

"Well, whoever it is, they're getting an axe in the head!" roared Draxian.

Then, as one, the group turned to face the mountain looming in the distance and paused.

"So… we're doing this, then?" Silas questioned with a sigh.

"We *have* to," replied Elysia as she looked around at her comrades. "… ready?"

"Adventure song! Someone sing an adventure song!" Draxian looked expectantly around at the group. "No? Gah, you're all useless. I knew we should have brought a Bard!"

Kelebor shook his head and smiled. "How long until The Weeping Vale, Silas? Will we make it before nightfall?"

"About twenty miles, so no, we'll need to make camp before then," Silas replied, looking off into the distance. "If we set off now, I'm sure I can find us a suitable spot before we enter the vale."

At first, the four walked in silence.

Around them, the corruption became subtly more apparent… It started with wilted wildflowers by the roadside, birdsong thinning to silence, and a strange weight in the air like a storm refusing to break. Before long, trees leaned unnaturally, their bark blistered and black. Rotten horse carcasses and partially decaying human remains littered the treeline on either side of the path.

Kelebor glanced down at a small corpse, what could only once have been a child, and gagged at the smell.

"Did the curse from the mountain do this?" Kelebor said, holding back the urge to vomit. "It's hideous."

"I didn't think it would have been this bad…" Draxian muttered. "It looks like they slaughtered each other. Madness…"

Trying to lighten the mood, Elysia spoke up. "Kelebor, tell me about your magic. I'm curious how it all works."

"Oh. Didn't they explain it in your sanctum, Elysia?"

"Only a little. We only really ever learned about prayer and study, though," Elysia replied. "I think they didn't want us getting distracted with the outside world. The first time I ever saw someone from the Silvered Guild was when Drax, Silas and I arrived there looking for help. When we met you."

Kelebor glanced downwards again, remembering the day like it was yesterday. The accident, volunteering for adventure with a random trio of adventures. As he looked down, he glimpsed another putrid corpse.

"Don't look down there!" Elysia almost snapped. "So. Tell me, how does it all work?"

Kelebor sighed and glanced up at her. "You don't feel it, do you? The drain. The *cost*…" He ran his hand through the silver strands of his hair. "Every time I cast; it *takes*. Not energy, not mana or whatever some people think. It takes... *me.*"

Elysia said nothing, just listened.

"I used to have dark hair. All of it. I thought I could control it... Then...T-Th..." Kelebor winced at the memory.

Elysia reached out and touched his arm. "It's OK."

"It's not. I...I... *killed* people. My magic did, I mean. I just couldn't control it. That's how I got this first one," Kelebor said, pointing to a strand of bright silver hair. His hand visibly shaking at the memory. "It was an accident, I swear. They were going to cast me out - exile me from the Silvered Guild so I agreed to come with you to redeem myself and prove I can control this power. Control myself."

The three goblins... was that control?

"I'm sure you can. You are still young," Elysia said reassuringly. "It's a very brave thing you did - agreeing to come with three strangers."

"Thanks, I guess. Although, I'm twenty-one, but I look about twenty-eight, maybe thirty. Every spell ages us and the stronger the spell, the bigger the drain."

"Do the silver strands come with every spell you cast?" Elysia wondered.

"No. Just wild spells - powerful spells that push us beyond our normal limits," Kelebor said, as he let out a sigh. "I can cast smaller spells at only a minimal cost, but these two strands of silver I have are from times where I lost control. When I let the magic control me, instead. I don't see them as power. They're a mark of shame."

"That's why folk call them Ashbloods," Draxian interrupted, speaking with a mouthful of dried meat. "Some of the most powerful mages have a full head of ash silver hair. One big spell away from croaking it."

Elysia glared over at Draxian before she continued with Kelebor. "But your magic is stronger now, isn't it? Every wild spell increases your power?"

Kelebor gave a bleak smile. "Yeah, stronger. More chaotic. Closer to the end."

"… and there's no way to undo it?" Elysia frowned.

"It's not a curse. It's a *cost*," he said. "Real magic, *arcane magic*, burns from the inside out. We bargain years for power. Some give them all at once and vanish in a blaze whilst others, like me, try to pay in slow drips."

Elysia meekly touched the holy symbol on her breastplate. "My power doesn't do that."

"I know." Kelebor's voice was soft, but there was something behind it. Not envy exactly, but something close. "Your power is given. Mine is *stolen*."

Kelebor paused.

"One day, I'll cast my final spell. I hope it will be beautiful and I pray it will do some good… but then… it'll kill me."

"That day is a long way away yet, my human friend," said Silas.

"I hope so."

"You'll be great!" Draxian said, patting him on the back. "I'm glad you're with us and I promise I won't give you a hard time about the crispy green-skins back there. You did good. Don't be too hard on yourself. It was you or them."

Up above, the sun vanished behind thick, black clouds.

"I think it's time we set up camp," Silas said. "It's only going to get rougher the further we go."

"Sounds good to me!" Draxian clapped his hands together. "Let's get a fire going. I'm starving!"

The group, led by Silas, left the path and moved into the

treeline for some protection and began to settle in for the night. Silas set up a small and discrete fire, surrounded by large stones found on the side of the road, and they ate their travel rations heartily. In silence.

In the dark, the looming presence of Valkyr's Rise seemed even more imposing, as blue and purple energy crackled from the summit. "What do you suppose it's like up there?" Wondered Kelebor to the group, staring up at the mountain.

"Just a problem for tomorrow," Draxian smiled. "Get some sleep, laddie. I'll keep first watch."

The thought of sleep seemed so distant for Kelebor - his first day outside the walls of the guild didn't exactly go as planned. The companions he was traveling with seemed like good people, though. He thought he would be in for a night of tossing and turning but the second his head hit the bedroll, sleep took him.

Kelebor awoke, standing at the base of the mountain as it bled. From its peak, rivers of black ichor ran down the mountainside like veins, steaming and pulsing with a heartbeat that wasn't his. Kelebor stood at the base, looking up, barefoot in ash.

He couldn't move. Couldn't breathe.

Something *watched* him.

"You burn so bright... but you are so small."

Kelebor tried to run, but his legs sank into the ash. His hands were aflame with his arcane fire. It licked up his arms, peeling away his skin.

He screamed, and the mountain laughed.

"You'll never be enough."

"You'll die *trying*."

"*They* will all die!"

Kelebor jolted awake with a ragged gasp, hands clutching at his chest. A faint burn blackened his palms. He looked down at his hands in horror.

"Was I channeling a spell in my sleep?" he whispered to himself. *"I could have killed everyone!"*

He glanced around at the others, checking if they were OK, but Silas was missing. Kelebor squinted in the darkness but couldn't make out anything outside the glow of the fading campfire. Then, out of nowhere, he felt a hand on his shoulder. "Keep quiet," whispered Silas, scanning the surrounding darkness, bow in his other hand. "We have company…wake the others, but do it *quietly.*"

Kelebor stood to move over to Elysia when an arrow whizzed past his head and thunked into a tree.

"We're under attack! To arms!" Silas roared, rapidly firing three arrows into the black. Something in the darkness made a wet gurgling sound and flopped to the floor.

Draxian vaulted up to his feet and roared, his eyes wide with excitement. Elysia clutched her mace and turned to guard their rear.

And Kelebor… did *nothing.* He couldn't even see what was happening around him outside the light of the campfire - his human eyes straining in the dark. He looked down at his blackened hands and wondered what would have happened if he didn't wake from the dream…

Draxian's axe intercepted two figures in black leather as they charged into the campfire light, leaping over a rock with curved daggers in hand. The axe caught the first assassin in the collarbone and cleaved downwards to cut the second from shoulder to sternum. The two attackers screamed and fell into a heap.

Kelebor looked down at the twitching bodies. They were humans… just humans. But from where?

With his eyes watching the gargling, writhing assassins on the floor, Kelebor missed the one sneaking up behind Elysia and in a flash; it had his arms around Elysia from behind, curved knife at her throat.

"We have you n…."

Elysia gasped, having zero interest in hearing the rest of the taunt, and swung her mace upwards and over her shoulder to catch the assassin - caving in his face. As the assassin staggered backwards, dropping the blade, Elysia turned and struck again - this time square in the chest. It hit with such holy fury that the assailant's eye sockets burned, sending him tumbling to the floor, his mind totally consumed by divine fire.

She glanced at Kelebor. "We need you! Come on, help us."

It felt like the dream again.

Unable to move.

Consumed by fear.

Out of no-where, another assassin leaped from a nearby rock and pinned Elysia to the floor, knocking her mace from her grasp - sending it spinning away before landing in the mud. His blade cut deep into her shoulder, squelching as it sliced through skin and muscle.

"Argghh!" Elysia screamed in pain and flailed her arms up in a weak attempt to remove the assailant, but it was no good.

Kelebor was ready. This was it. The fire spell clung to the tip of his tongue, heat gathering in his chest. All he had to do was *breathe*. Speak the word. *Let it go.*

He didn't.

He *couldn't*.

The assassin, now nose to nose with Elysia, grinned and slid his blackened tongue across her cheek, like licking meat juices off a finger. The blade now cutting deeper into her flesh.

"Get...Off...ME," Elysia yelled.

"Mmm, I love the taste of priestess. So sweet. Maybe I'll t..."

Silas's arrow took the assassin through the neck.

Blood sprayed across Kelebor's face as the gargling body fell on Elysia, twitching like a fish, blood spurting over her pristine breastplate.

"Pull yourself together," Silas growled. "He almost took Elysia!" Then vanished into the trees again.

Elysia pushed the body onto the floor, rose to her feet and healed her wound. "Kelebor!" she shouted. "Cast!"

"I... I can't."

Elysia's gaze locked on him for a breath, a thousand thoughts behind her eyes. Then she picked up her mace from the mud and turned back to the battle. But they were gone. Vanished into the darkness as quickly as they had appeared.

"Arg, come back and fight you cowards!" Draxian's rage was still brewing strong.

Once everything was calm, Silas began marching over to Kelebor, about to unleash a torrent of abuse, but for Elysia resting a hand on his chest. "It's OK, brother."

"OK? You almost had it. If Kel..." Silas fumed.

"It's OK, Silas," Elysia smiled that smile again. "I'm sure next time, Kelebor will be ready."

Silas glared at Kelebor, as if to "say *you better be*," then turned to face The Weeping Vale that lay before them.

"I-... I-I'm sorry," Kelebor said as he sat on a nearby log. "I just couldn't..."

"Sun's rising. Let's get going." Silas ordered, not even able to look at Kelebor.

The four hastily packed up the camp and marched into The Weeping Vale, as the smell of the rotting fields and black, charred earth filled their nostrils.

Brimholt didn't earn its nickname 'The Weeping Vale' because it wept like a grieving wife, mourning the loss of their beloved husband. It wept like a corpse, still gasping through the last dregs of breath. It was foul and fetid, long removed of life.

Each step they took squelched.

Silas crouched, lowered a hand to the ground and whispered, "I can feel it. It's not just decay. It's despair. This land is sick."

Kelebor said nothing. He walked with his head low, avoiding their eyes, trying to clean his blackened hands on his robe, still haunted by the dream, the ambush... and his failure.

"Kelebor," Silas stood and suddenly snapped. "If anything happens again, you *will* act. Or we'll leave you behind." The words, out of nowhere, cut through the vale like a blade.

Kelebor flinched. "...I said I was sorry."

"'Sorry' doesn't stop a blade from cutting deep. 'Sorry' doesn't stop my sister from nearly losing her life. 'Sorry' doesn't stop me from nearly losing everything!"

Elysia stepped between them. "That's enough."

"No," Silas growled, his voice rising. "We're walking into a cursed pit of foul things. In a land surrounded by death and decay and we're dragging a dead weight."

Kelebor clenched his fists, his face flushed red with rage and shame. "You think I *want* to freeze up? Like it's a choice? Tell me, have you ever burned yourself from the inside just to save someone?"

"I've saved many people and earned many scars. Maybe you should try it sometime," Silas hissed. "Instead of hiding behind excuses and one or two *bad dreams*."

"It wasn't just a bad dream..." Kelebor growled.

"Like a child having a nightmare, wanting his mother," Silas spat. "You're pathetic."

"I almost cast in my sleep!"

"Good! I wish you did. At least then your magic may have actually done something useful, for once."

"Enough!" Elysia shouted, glaring at the both of them. "Both of you!"

Even Draxian turned, eyebrows raised, fingers twitching on the haft of his axe.

The silence that followed was almost... *too* silent.

No wind.

No breath.

"This is not *us*," she whispered, glancing around. "It is *this place.*"

The realization passed between them like lightning.

She glanced up to the summit of Valkyr's Rise, "It is *him*," she said. "Reaching out... twisting us. It's the madness that caused all those corpses on the road. We can't let it take us too." Up at the summit, blue and purple lightning crackled outwards into the clouds, like lightning retreating.

Draxian exhaled through his nose. "Then let's not wait around to see who it turns next. We're almost at the base."

Silas stepped back, shaking his head. "I... I'm sorry," he muttered. "I don't know why I reacted like that."

"You were not *yourself*," Elysia said firmly. "Our quest is over already if we turn on each other now."

The four continued walking, squelching their way towards the base of the mountain.

The wind howled through the clefts of Valkyr's Rise, biting at skin and spirit alike. Above them, the mountain loomed, a black monolith of jagged stone and creeping mist - its peak lost in swirling dark clouds like the lid of a sealed tomb.

"It looks so big now that we're here." Kelebor said, craning his neck upwards to look at the peak. "...too big."

"Hey, at least there's a path!" Draxian shouted, pointing at a nearby trail carved into the rock. "Can't be that bad if there's a path!"

"Let's get this over and done with," Silas muttered, as he slung his bow over his shoulder. "Follow me."

The path was narrow and crumbling and hostile, lined with sharp stones that tore at boots and calves. Every step sapped the energy, as if they were growing heavier the higher they climbed. On the mountainside, nothing grew. Just ash and sulfur... and dread. When they finally stopped to rest, behind a leaning spire of shattered granite, silence hung heavier than the mist, but the air was almost unbreathable.

Kelebor stared as his hands, still blackened. Some stains are impossible to clean completely. "This is madness... I'm not strong enough. I'm sorry everyone, I should never have come." His voice was barely more than a rasp. "I freeze up. People die."

Elysia sat with her holy symbol gripped in white-knuckled fists, looking around at her party members struggling to catch their breath. "No," she whispered. "I saw the vision. I thought it was a calling." Her voice cracked. "What if it's not? What if it's a trap, and I led us into it? Look around us. This place is beyond our help. What can we do here?" Elysia doubled up and coughed up jet black mucus as the soot, ash and god knows what else filled her nostrils.

Silas didn't sit. He stood behind his sister, staring down at her. "God damn it, El. I told myself I came to protect you," he murmured. "But I can't. Not from this place. Not from the Gods, or fate, or your own heart." His knuckles whitened on the grip of his bow.

Draxian was the last to speak. He leaned on his axe, breathing hard, a smear of dried blood still on his cheek. "You know… all my life I've chased glory," he said. "But maybe I'm just a loud fool with a big axe…"

Silence again. Only the wind replied, shrieking through the broken teeth of the mountain. Elysia finally looked up, wiping her nose. "Should we turn back?"

No one answered. Because the truth was that none of them knew what was waiting at the summit.

Was it a God?

A prison?

A lie?

Maybe all of it. Maybe none.

Kelebor's mind flashed back to the guild. If he went back now, he'd be a failure… He swallowed hard and said, "If we turn back… who else will come? Who will unearth this mystery?"

Silas didn't move, but his voice was like steel drawn from a sheath, as he closed his eyes and said with a sigh, "No one."

"…who will save this land down there?" Kelebor continued, pointing down to The Weeping Vale. "We've come so far. One way or the other, we have to see this through."

Elysia stood, slowly. "Yes." Her legs trembling. "He's right. We have to see this through. I must have been shown this vision for a reason…"

Kelebor thought, for once, it was Elysia who needed a comforting hand, her faith wavering, and so reached out to touch her arm. "I believe you, Elysia. We are here with you."

She locked eyes with Kelebor and they both shared a soft smile.

Silas glared at the physical contact between the two. Jealousy overwhelmed him, but this feeling went beyond protective sibling instincts; *it was something else.*

Draxian gave a bitter grunt, which snapped Silas out of his gaze. "Well, what are we waiting for? I say we get up there, decapitate the bastard in charge, save the God and be on our way."

"Wise words," Silas said. "…for a Dwarf."

Draxian chuckled and said, "Come on. Just think how good the ale will taste when we get back! First round is on the Elf."

The mist thickened as they climbed as the wind grew colder. Each step towards the apocalyptic blue and purple sky above growing harder and more daunting.

Up there, *he* waited.

As they crested the final ridge… and the world *broke.* The summit was a crater of black obsidian and shattered bone and at the center loomed *him.* Not a man. Not a beast. Not a known God.

Something else.

Its giant form shifted. Easily two hundred feet high, thrashing around in agony. Wings of smoke, limbs too long and too many, flickering between shapes that the eye refused to track. Its face, if it could be called that, was a spiraling maw of light and void, surrounded by halos of twitching bone. To look directly at it was to feel your memories bleed, your faith in reality to buckle. Chains of roaring lightning, blue and purple, bound it to the mountain's jagged heart, driven deep into obsidian pylons. But even bound, it pulsed with impossible gravity.

Elysia fell to her knees. "I… I can't. It's wrong. It's *wrong.* I didn't dream this… This is a nightmare."

Draxian winced and said, "What is it? This is no God!"

"I… I've seen nothing like it… There are no texts in the

libraries of the guild which talk of such a creature," Kelebor replied. "Elysia, what do we do?"

Silas sighed. "No. This *is* a God," he said, lifting Elysia carefully to her feet. "Just not of this world. It is from the old world. Elves used to tell stories about such beings to their children."

"Well, what's it doing here?! Old world stuff should stay in the old world!" Draxian wondered.

"Silas. why would The Lightmother want me to free... *this?*" Elysia questioned, turning to her brother. "Surely we can't unleash this on the world!"

Around the ancient God stood a ring of black-robed figures, similar to the assassins who attacked the camp. However, these were no assassins but unholy cultists, chanting as one, with tongues split down the middle. Intermixed with the ring of cultists, there were pink-skinned beings, which almost undulated with an inhuman movement. "Ugh, what are those disgusting pink things?" Draxian asked, pointing to the strange figures writhing in the distance.

"Demon Spawn," Silas explained as he drew his bow in preparation. "Creatures birthed from raw pain and madness. Twisted by the God's torment. It seems the cultists have enslaved them to do their will." The Demon Spawn's bodies were spindly and malformed, skin stretched too tight over jutting bones and plates of mottled chitin. Some were walking upright, whilst others scuttled or slithered across the rock.

"Hmph. Can they be killed?" Draxian asked the only question he cared to know the answer to.

"Yes," Silas nodded. "They're not born. They have leaked from the God's dreaming mind and enslaved by these Humans. They can be killed like anything else"

Just then, the air cracked.

The God turned and *saw* them.

A voice, or maybe a thought, slithered into their skulls with a deafening volume.

I am Shaldreth.

Free me.

Burn for me.

Obey.

The chanting stopped as the cultists turned to face the intruders and began unsheathing curved blades. Beside them, the Demon Spawn snapped their heads towards the group and shrieked.

Silas readied his bow. "This is it. We need to eliminate the cultists and then work out what to do with *that* thing."

Elysia drew her mace. "No turning back now. The Lightmother is with us…"

Kelebor looked at his hands. "I am ready. Whatever the cost. You can count on me."

Draxian simply ran towards the cultists and shouted, "Now THIS is glory!"

The air split open with a shriek as the cultists and the Demon Spawn surged forward to meet the invaders, who interrupted their ritual. Draxian bellowed and threw himself into the charging demons, axe whirling, cleaving through demon flesh with sprays of black blood. One latched onto his shoulder, biting down deep - its teeth like jagged shards of glass. Instinctively, he shoulder-barged into a stone outcrop, crushing the demon's skull between Dwarf and rock, and howled with pain and triumph.

Silas' arrows punched through black-robed throats, his fingers moving faster than thought, but for every cultist that fell, two more from behind took their place.

"Keep it up. Don't let them push us back," Silas ordered, firing another three shots in a blur. "We have to hold here!"

Elysia called down radiant fire, her voice raw with divine strain, but the light dimmed around her as Shaldreth's presence pressed in - warping, weakening, *corrupting*.

"Argh, my mind." Elysia cried, as she dropped her mace and clutched her head. "That thing is… fighting me."

Free me.

Free me.

Free me.

"It's so powerful." Kelebor yelled as he felt the chaos from Shaldreth too. "We can't stay here! It's too much!"

Up ahead, Draxian and Silas were dispatching the foes with relative ease, humans and demons alike… but it wasn't enough. More kept coming. Silas glanced backwards to witness Kelebor and Elysia huddled together, their minds totally wracked with pain. "Drax!" Silas called out to his Dwarven ally. "Shaldreth is corrupting those two. We need to save them!"

Draxian didn't hear. He was too busy.

The mountain shuddered as the ancient God writhed, every twitch of its bound form sending waves of agony through the air. The chains of lightning strained, and each crack of energy was like a scream of a forgotten tongue. Every second they lingered in the presence of the being, the more the world *bent...* Time itself seemed to twist in an unfathomable fashion, bending around the ancient being known only as Shaldreth.

Elysia staggered, clutching her head. "It's too much. His pain. He's screaming inside! I can't focus!"

"I'm here, Elysia. I'm here," Kelebor said as a wave of chaos washed over him. "Arrg, we need to go! I can't stand this anymore!"

Silas fired two shots simultaneously into the chest of an on-rushing cultist. "We can't free it! It's madness! It'll tear the world apart!"

In a moment of calm, Draxian turned, panting, slick with blood. "Then what? We die here? For *nothing?*"

Kelebor stood at the edge of battle, paralyzed... *again.* His hands trembling, eyes wide with fear and disbelief. He had trained his whole life - studied ancient tomes, endured sleepless years of lessons and pain and volunteered for this mission for atonement, but nothing had prepared him for this sight. The God's mind clawed at his. *It knew him.* Knew his shame, his fear, his fragile hope. And it *fed* on it as another wave of demons and cultists attacked.

Up ahead, Silas screamed as demon claws tore through his side. Draxian fell to one knee, surrounded by black robes. If those two warriors fell, Elysia and Kelebor would soon follow. All would be lost...

"I'm useless," he muttered. "I'll get them killed, just like... just like..."

A weak hand gripped his shoulder. Elysia. Her eyes locked onto his. "You will not," she said. "You are here, with us. That means something. We have to destroy it. We need to stop Shaldreth. We can do this... together." Her hand squeezing ever so gently as she spoke that last word.

Together.

Kelebor's heart thundered. His hands burned. He raised his hands to the storm and realized that, this time, the cost would be worth it.... And the magic *tore* through him.

Kelebor channeled... Every single hair on his head turned white as snow. Wrinkles spread out across his face, like arcing lightning. His bones screamed as power rushed in like a floodgate shattered. The words poured from him; a lost tongue summoned from the void of time. As a jet of pure iridescent arcane light shot from his fingertips into the sky.

And above… The clouds *exploded.*

With a roar that shook the heavens, a void opened overhead and out of it came tearing another being of the old world - a great, Golden Dragon - mighty and ancient. Light poured from its eyes and mouth with molten, furious justice. "Kelebor, what are you doing?" Elysia shouted - her voice barely audible over the chaos, as Kelebor stumbled backwards, seemingly unsure of what he had just unleashed.

The dragon dived and struck the God like a meteor, slamming into it. Claws opened, like an eagle diving for a fish. As the two collided, a shockwave knocked everyone at the summit off their feet. They were just pawns here. No match for claw and fang and shadow.

The chains binding Shaldreth to the mountain top snapped. Purple lightning from the pylons whipped outwards and caught a handful of cultists, instantly burning them to cinders. The mountaintop, unable to contain two such titans, cracked, stone splitting like bark under lightning. An abyss opened in front of Shaldreth - Down into the mountain and below, causing cultists and Demon Spawn to be flung into the void.

The party could only watch, helpless, clinging to a nearby rock, as the two titans grappled. Then… with one last roar, they tumbled, locked in fury, over the edge of the abyss and down into the very mountain itself. Into depths unknown. Down, down, into the misted abyss below.

Gone.

Draxian and Silas took this opportunity to finish the remaining cultists and Demon Spawn, who avoided the fall.

Then… it was over.

The wind returned.

The curse lifted, as if the mountain, at last, could breathe again.

Elysia collapsed to her knees, trembling. Silas coughed up blood as he clutched the wound at his side, looking over at Kelebor in awe. Draxian leaned on his axe, like it was the only thing holding him up.

Kelebor, now gray and hollow-eyed, looked to the sky as the void closed. "I did it," he whispered.

"Did what?" Elysia gasped, her eyes wide with shock. "What did you do?"

"I saved everyone," answered Kelebor, nonchalantly. "The magic inside me *wanted* to be cast. The words *needed* to be said… So I said them."

"That's not control, Kelebor! You gave in to the magic. It sounds like you sent a plea out to the other gods of old?" Silas shouted with an equal measure of rage and disbelief.

"I…Yes." Kelebor replied. "I did."

"Well… Someone listened." Draxian said, stumbling back to the group.

"Or something…" Elysia pondered, as she muttered under her breath. "So the other old Gods… still watch. Was this what we were supposed to do, though?"

"The power answered me," Kelebor mumbled. "But it wasn't just a spell. Something… *else* out there… listened."

"You had us worried for a minute there, Kel," Draxian said, as he gave the mage a playful push. "Thought you were going to freeze up again."

"Maybe it would have been better if he had…" Silas said as

he still seethed with rage. "What was the cost this time?"

Elysia looked around at the scene. Bodies, both human and demon, lay strewn across the mountainside. Her eyes locked onto the large pylons, now devoid of lightning, and said, "Did we destroy him?" The wind whispered again atop Valkyr's Rise - like it was catching its breath after some long, dreadful thing.

Elysia stood at the abyss' edge, staring down into the mist-choked hole where god and dragon had fallen. Her holy symbol, now scorched at the edges, felt heavier than ever. "Why me?" she thought. "Why this quest? Why now?"

Kelebor stood alone, his silver-white hair wild in the moun-tain wind, eyes rimmed in dark hollows. The spell had changed him. *Cracked* something inside him open, but only time would tell what that was.

They all looked up as thunder rumbled across the horizon, but this wasn't a storm. They saw wings and a flash of gold - the ancient gold dragon still lived.

"Look, the dragon! It must have escaped the abyss." Silas supposed.

"Er, that can't be good," Draxian exclaimed. "There hasn't been a dragon around here for hundreds of years." The four of them stared into the distance as the golden flash flew from view. What havoc would that now wreak against the world?

And what of Shaldreth? Was it bested down in the abyss? Or does that too still live on? No one could say. Beneath all the questions rising in their minds, there pulsed one final, inescapable truth:

The Gods of the old world were stirring.

Not just one.

Not just here.

Across the land, eyes were opening.

...and this age would not be ready.

About the Author

Based on England's south coast, Daniel Kipps lives with his family and pet dog. Daniel enjoys creating slow burn, Lovecraftian inspired stories, which build dread and make the reader feel uneasy before finishing with a large, action-filled, horrific climax. He will soon start work on his first full novel, based on the world created in 'Whispers Beneath the Mountain'.

Thank you for reading this book. I hope you enjoyed it and if you ever want to reach out, you can find my social links, email and official website below.

Daniel@Danielkipps.com

You can connect with me on:
- https://danielkipps.com
- https://x.com/KippsDaniel